CK HOLMES
MYSTERY MAGAZINE

VOLUME 1, NUMBER 1   WINTER 2008

Features

Fiction

Sherlock Holmes Classic

Cartoons

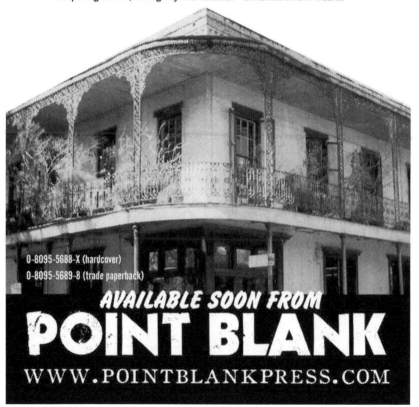

FROM WATSON'S SCRAPBOOK

When it comes to acts of hubris, *Sherlock Holmes Mystery Magazine* might well earn its staff assignment to the lower ridges and clefts of Mt. Purgatorio. After all, it is published in America, where aficionados of the Great Detective call themselves Sherlockians, not Holmesians, as we do in England. Whereas I have had my share of pleasant encounters socially and professionally with the Baker Street Irregulars (BSI), Holmes bridles at what he has termed "characteristic Yankee familiarities," and therefore these pages will embrace the adjective employed on this side of the Atlantic pond: *Holmesian.*

When I began chronicling my friend's career, I had no idea my efforts would ultimately engender a host of adaptations, and sometimes distortions. My business agent, a Scottish gentleman named Sir Arthur Conan Doyle, was unable to stem this flood of inaccuracies, so let me set the record straight on a few points.

First, a long overdue confession: Conan Doyle, a splendid novelist who on occasion effectively assumed the role of detective himself, had *considerable* to do with writing up and polishing my case notes!

Next, this slanderous business concerning Holmes's use of drugs . . . it is a fact that my friend used to injected himself with a seven per cent cocaine solution of cocaine, and although it is a habit that I, as a physician, deplore, please understand that in those days it was neither illegal nor even deemed socially disreputable. Holmes abandoned the practice altogether, but let me also point out that his seven per solution was comparatively mild. A therapeutic dose of cocaine in those days was set by British pharmacologists at *ten* per cent. Another nettle is Irene Adler . . . nothing infuriates Holmes more than to be portrayed mooning about like a love-struck adolescent. Romantics pounce upon that line I wrote in *A Scandal in Bohemia*: "To Sherlock Holmes she is always *the* woman." But apparently they skip over the paragraph

"My goodness! Your dear old uncle seems to have left everything to me!"

that directly follows —

> "It was not that he felt any emotion akin to love for Irene Adler. All emotions, and that one particularly, were abhorrent to his cold, precise, but admirably balanced mind. He was the most perfect reasoning and observing machine that the world has seen: but he never spoke of the softer passions save with a gibe and a sneer."

Now, gentle reader, can you tell me the street address of the rooms that I shared with Sherlock Holmes? Many Holmesians (and probably most of the 'Sherlockians') would reply, "221 B Baker Street?" But you see, Holmes and I lived one flight up in *Apartment B*. Thus, our proper street address was 221 Baker Street.

In spite of these noted exceptions, I generally enjoy the Holmes pastiches, plays and films. It irritates both Holmes and Mrs Hudson that I am often portrayed as a bumbling Colonel Blimp, but I don't really mind. The royalties elicited from producers buffer my pride marvelously. As for Holmes, he has scant tolerance for actors who play him, though he has the grace not to mention names. Yet for all that, he has a prima donna's ego and when pressed, begrudgingly admits his manner and inflection were effectively captured by Mr. Rathbone.

Well, now, I've had my say for this issue, so I shall turn over the residuum of this column to the editor, Mr. Kaye.

— John H. Watson, M. D.

It is both a pleasure and a heavy responsibility to assume the editorial duties of a second Wildside Press periodical, the first being *H. P. Lovecraft's Magazine of Horror,* now approaching its third issue (or rather, fourth, since we actually did an issue 1.5 as a special extra for subscribers.) This magazine is an assignment I relish, though I am well aware that I am perhaps standing in for that peerless Holmesian scholar, the distinguished Parker College (PA) professor J. Adrian Fillmore, whose intimate knowledge of the mind and character of Sherlock Holmes led him to edit the St. Martin's Press anthologies, *The Resurrected Holmes* and *The Confidential Casebook of Sherlock Holmes.* Unfortunately, Professor Fillmore is on an extended sabbatical and cannot even be reached by e-mail; some concern has been expressed about his health since his own Holmesian adventures, but a recent communiqué from the estimable Professor Harold Shea assures us that Fillmore is still actively involved in new literary worlds and vistas. (Regrettably, Shea could not resist a gratuitous observation about his colleague: "*Gad, what a name!*")

My own contributions to Holmesian literature began in 1971

Ben Perkins is back!

It feels so good to say that.

Twenty-three years ago, when Rob Kantner introduced his Detroit PI in the short story "C Is for Cookie," he probably had no idea he was heralding in a new era of mystery fiction.

Before Rob, the private eye genre was glutted with down-in-their-luck losers who wore trench coats and talked like Bogart. Stereotypes ruled the paperback racks, and a revamp was sorely needed. Rob's genius was to give his hero something more than clichéd one-liners and a drinking problem. Namely, a life." *J. A. Konrath*

This collection includes 18 stories featuring Ben Perkins, from the earliest part of his career to the latest chapter. The final story, "Sex and Violins" has never before been published.

TROUBLE IS WHAT I DO

Collected Ben Perkins stories

Rob Kantner

HARDCOVER $34.00 ISBN: 0809511576
TRADE PAPERBACK $19.95 ISBN:0809511568
360 PAGES

when Luther Norris published a now-rare edition of 300 copies of *The Histrionic Holmes,* my study of the Great Detective's acting skills, which brought a most gratifiying encomium from the late great John Dickson Carr. In 1979, Holmes played a role of some importance in my humorous fantasy, *The Incredible Umbrella,* but came front and center in 1994 when I edited a large Holmesian anthology, *The Game is Afoot,* for St. Martin's Press, a book followed by the two above-cited works that Professor Fillmore's labours helped bring about. I also wrote and produced a play of the same title as my first anthology, and my theatre company, The Open Book, is helping to produce Carole Buggé's new musical, *Sherlock Holmes.*

My non-Holmesian credits include five Hilary Quayle and two Marty Gold mystery novels; teaching mystery writing for more than twenty years at New York University (am very proud of the many students who entered the profession and sold successful novels and at least one screenplay); serving as a judge for the Edgar Awards of the Mystery Writers of America, and chairman of the judging committee for many years for the Nero Award offered by The Wolfe Pack, the national Nero Wolfe society.

S*herlock Holmes Mystery Magazine* has a few things in common with *H.P. Lovecraft's Magazine of Horror:* both are quarterlies, both pay homage to two famous genre names, but neither are limited to pastiches and parodies of their titular progenitors. While *Sherlock Holmes Mystery Magazine* will always reverence the Holmesian Canon, the mutual intention of its editor and publisher is to create a new mystery magazine with as great a scope as its contributors enable us to offer.

Thus, while Watsonian pastiches and spoofs will appear as often as the merit of such submissions deserve, they will be counterbalanced by new mystery stories, period pieces, tales of murder and other crimes, puzzle/riddle tales if anyone still writes them, and in short, mysteries set in the present, past, and possibly even the future. Science fiction is less likely in these pages, but superior SF crime stories and mysteries have been written by authors such as Isaac Asimov, Alfred Bester, Lloyd Biggle, Ray Bradbury, and Harry Harrison, so I plan to keep an open mind about this.

When I was a Nero Award judge and since then, I have become increasingly concerned that today's mystery novels are really crime stories. To me, a genuine mystery story is one that provides clues and red herrings, is reader-solvable (or at least creates that illusion!); that is, in short, an example of the fiction championed by Arthur Conan Doyle (sometimes!), by Rex Stout, Ellery Queen, Craig Rice, Clayton Rawson, Agatha Christie, John

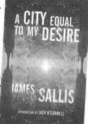

Dickson Carr, etc. I am afraid that modern writers have either grown lazy, or are at a loss as to the techniques of forging sleuth-driven mysteries . . . a term I am gratified to attribute to the publisher of *Sherlock Holmes Mystery Magazine*, John Betancourt, who is himself a thoroughly capable mystery writer.

I worry that we will not receive submissions of the old school of mystery, though even if we do, *Sherlock Holmes Mystery Magazine* will strive not to earn any labels like "retro" or "throwback." We will never exclude that excellent writing that so many of the newer authors are capable of (I am especially impressed by Lia Matera).

What I hope to create is a balanced mix of mystery fiction and articles, highlighting, I hope, what Ellery Queen once called the "Grand Old Game."

I hope that the contents of this initial issue constitute a modest attempt to exemplify our hopes for the shape, direction and future of *Sherlock Holmes Mystery Magazine*. In addition to insights into issues both Holmesian and ratiocinative from our estimable columnists Kim Newman and Lenny Picker, the nonfiction portion of *Sherlock Holmes Mystery Magazine Vol. 1, No. 1* includes an interview of the awesomely prolific Ron Goulart and a letters column by no less a personage than Sherlock Holmes's landlady Mrs Hudson, who fervently hopes that readers of this first issue will write to her promptly about any care and concern of the heart, head, stomach or wherever, for as she puts it, "One grows with the times, and what a relief to escape the strictured mores of the Victorian and Edwardian eras. I doubt, though, that dear Dr Watson shares my views." (Yes, she and Watson . . . and of course, Holmes . . . still live. But *didn't you know that?*)

For those readers (if such exist) who are not familiar with the original sixty Sherlock Holmes adventures, cases and memoirs, *Sherlock Holmes Mystery Magazine* intends to reprint one each issue, beginning with *The "Gloria Scott,"* which was published in 1894 in the fourth Holmes book, and second of the short story collections, *The Memoirs of Sherlock Holmes*. The fourth of the tales in that volume, it is offered first in this magazine because it is, in effect, Sherlock Holmes's very first case.

The nautical theme of *The "Gloria Scott"* is echoed in the other Holmes tale in these pages. "The Strange Case of the Haunted Freighter," a brand new Holmes adventure with occult overtones that was written especially for *Sherlock Holmes Mystery Magazine* by Carole Buggé, author of numerous Sherlock Holmes tales, including two critically acclaimed novels, *The Star of India* and *The Haunting of Torre Abbey,* from St. Martin's

"Guess where I hid the armored car, boss!
No . . . No . . . No, guess again!"

Press; she is, in my estimation, the hands-down best Holmes pastiche writer since Ellery Queen's *A Study in Terror.*

This issue's non-Holmesian stories begins with *The Mystery of the Missing Automaton,* a new Harry Challenge mystery by Ron Goulart, and — odd coincidence! — a new Simon Ark case, *The Automaton Museum,* by Edward D. Hoch. Another bond of sorts between these stories is that though their detectives are to some extent associated with the fantasy genre, neither of these adventures cross over; they are genuine mysteries.

Hal Blythe's amusing puzzle with Holmesian undertones, *On the Heir,* is the first of a new series. Marc Bilgrey's *The Bet* is both a club story and a tale of murder, as is *Lost and Found,* one of the posthumous short stories of Jean Paiva, author of the highly re-

Publisher: *John Betancourt*

Editor: *Marvin Kaye*

Managing Editor: Stephen Segal

Assistant Editors: *P.D. Cacek, Sean Wallace*

Sherlock Holmes Mystery Magazine is published quarterly by Wildside Press, LLC. Sample copies: $9.95 (postage paid in the United States), $12.00 (postage paid elsewhere), from:

Wildside Press LLC
Subscription Dept.
9710 Traville Gateway Dr., #234
Rockville MD 20850

An electronic edition is available from
Fictionwise.com
www.fictionwise.com.

Writers' guidelines are available on the Wildside Press web site:

www.wildsidepress.com

Please do not send manuscripts to the publisher or they will be returned unread. All submissions must go to the editor at his New York address. While all reasonable care will be taken with unsolicited materials, you should never send out your only copy of a story.

garded horror novels, *The Lilith Factor* and *The Last Gamble.*

The second issue of *Sherlock Holmes Mystery Magazine Sherlock Holmes Mystery Magazine* is in its early stages of preparation, and is expected to feature a wicked riff by Kim Newman on *A Study in Scarlet* — from Col. Moran's point of view!

Till then, please send your thoughts and problems to Mrs Hudson . . . and if you wish to contribute new mystery fiction to *Sherlock Holmes Mystery Magazine,* by all means query me at this email address: <shmm@wildsidepress.com>.

Canonically Yours,
Marvin Kaye

"AFTER EXAMINING THE CLUES I'VE COME TO THE CONCLUSION THAT YOU NEED TO RETURN TO YOUR OWN SUB-GENRE."

BAKER STREET BROWSINGS

book reviews
by Kim Newman

- *The New Annotated Sherlock Holmes, ed. by Leslie S. Klinger, Norton, $75.00/£35.00*
- *Sherlock Holmes: The Hidden Years, ed. by Michael Kurland, St. Martin's Minotaur, $24.95*

As the title *The New Annotated Sherlock Holmes* indicates, this Norton edition is not the first time that Sir Arthur Conan Doyle's Holmes stories have been published in annotated form. Editor and annotater Leslie S. Klinger admits that the hundred-pound gorilla of the field is the late William S. Baring-Gould, whose *The Annotated Sherlock Holmes* (1967) remains one of the most battered and consulted volumes in my library (any writer considering a Victorian British setting should have this — it's full of good stuff like hansom cab fares and ladies' fashions). Norton's handsome set, two thick volumes in a sturdy case, even *looks* like my John Murray edition of the Baring-Gould, down almost to the weight of the paper and the smell of the ink. There are, however, significant differences between Klinger and Baring-Gould; devotees will have no cause to retire their old *Annotated* and replace them with the *New* one, though they will need both sets.

Baring-Gould gets all four novels and the 56 short stories into his two (sometimes one) thick volumes, while Klinger saves the four book-length adventures (need I specify? — *A Study in Scarlet*, *The Sign of the Four*, *The Hound of the Baskervilles* and *The Valley of Fear*) for an as-yet-undelivered third. Baring-Gould was far more interested in providing the real-world dates for the fictional events of the stories and arranged the stories in (debatable) order of internal chronology (he places *The Sign of the Four* after 'A Scandal in Bohemia', which Doyle plainly did not intend). Klinger arranges them as Doyle did when collecting the stories into his five collections, *The Adventures of Sherlock Holmes*, *The Memoirs of Sherlock Holmes*, *The Return of Sherlock Holmes*, *His Last Bow* and *The Case-Book of Sherlock Holmes*. As usual, even simple decisions aren't definitive: 'The Cardboard Box' appeared in the *Strand* magazine run of the *Memoirs* and the first impression of the British edition of the collection, but was dropped from the American and most subsequent British editions (perhaps because of its relative gruesomeness), but the story opens with an especially neat if irrelevant bit of deduction ('You are right, Watson, it does seem a most preposterous way of settling a dispute') which was lifted probably by Doyle and pasted into the book publication of 'The Resident Patient'.

Baring-Gould reproduces the type from the *Strand*, and notes differences between original and subsequent editions; Klinger usually relies on *copy* from the *Strand* but set in an easier-to-read font, also pointing up occasions where misprints or errors have been corrected. Norton present the notes in purplish-crimson, which makes it easier to distinguish between Doyle and Klinger, though this doesn't extend to introductory and supplementary essays (on things like guns, gambling and deadly snakes, all attached to stories which highlight these topics). It's easy to understand why Norton and Klinger have led with the short stories rather than the novels — of the four, only *Baskervilles* isn't strangled by its lengthy backstory — but Holmes and Watson, and their world, were introduced in the first two novels, which were written and published before the first set of stories and might well have been the beginning and the end of Holmes. The stories may show a certain decline in quality as the series progresses, with one or two 'remakes' of successful earlier tales (long-running TV series tend to do the same thing), but there are unmemorable efforts early on ('A Case of Identity', the third story, is much less impressive than the rest of the *Adventures*) and gems late in the day ('The Problem of Thor Bridge' has most of the old snap). Re-reading the entire oeuvre in one go isn't advisable, but pulling the book down and savouring the tales one a week or a month is a hugely reliable pleasure — they 'play' very well read aloud, and parents of children slightly too old for babyish books find them a wonderful excuse for melodrama (it's rarely remarked, but Doyle is a fond, funny prose-writer and gets a lot of laughs in performance).

The shared approach of Baring-Gould and Klinger is that both proceed from the premise that Holmes and Watson were real people, and that Watson's manuscripts were prepared for publication by Doyle. Doyle started this when he wrote in self-reflective moments as Holmes comments on Watson's published versions of his cases or Mycroft mentions that Sherlock has become more famous thanks to the publicity accorded by his 'Boswell', though he couldn't have foreseen how out of hand it would get. This means that there are two types of annotation: firstly, footnotes that explain or elucidate references that might have been obvious to the original readers but with time have become obscure, or sometimes references of matters of British geography, politics, culture or language Americans have never quite fathomed (eg: explaining what the Serpentine is, something as familiar to British readers as, say, a reference to Golden Gate or Central Park would be to Americans); and, secondly, attempts to rationalise 'errors' made by Watson (or Doyle) or to uncover the true identities of characters Watson is supposed to have disguised to avoid scandal (royals, politicians, society folk, etc). The first are helpful, the second are fun — though nearly a century of this sort of thing has, I think, tended unfairly to downgrade the real achievements of Doyle, who is often presented as clumsy, slapdash or evasive.

Very occasionally, this game needs to be set aside, and Klinger is rather better than Baring-Gould at that. His footnotes don't have that slightly grumpy tone — and he frequently phrases them in the form of questions, not objecting to veracity but to credibility. I often sense that Sherlockians feel a certain frustration and resentment that Doyle didn't care about such things as calendar dates, continuity and dovetailing fictional and real-world events — but he was writing in a period before the evolution of that style. He cites names, dates and places to make his fictions seem convincing — as Wilkie Collins had done or Bram Stoker would do — but feels no obligation to make them names, dates and places that can be verified by old maps, newspapers and the *Dictionary of National Biography*. Baring-Gould comes close to kicking some stories out of the Canon simply because he can't make sense of the dates, which Klinger never does — he points out when a date given in the text as a Wednesday was actually a Friday but leaves it at that, and adds a chart at the back in a tentative attempt to put the stories in order. Overlooked in this are some things that interest me more than whether Lord Bellinger of 'The Second Stain' is supposed to be Gladstone or Salisbury. There are rarely notes that speculate on Doyle's specific inspirations — these stories came from somewhere, and it might be interesting to learn whether Doyle heard an anecdote or read a news item or chanced across a plot-nugget in general reading and then spun out a Holmes plot.

When we meet Holmes in 'A Scandal in Bohemia', Doyle takes care to reintroduce him for those unfamiliar with the two novels (which, originally, would have been most of the *Strand*'s readership) but — opening up a whole can of worms that has never satisfactorily been dealt with — he was also stuck with the ending of *The Sign of the Four*, when Watson leaves Baker Street to get married. Many adaptations of the series relegate Watson's marriage to a never-was-to-be timelines: both the Jeremy Brett and Ian Richardson versions have Watsons who don't connect with Mary Morstan and wistfully watch her leaving his life, then settling back into bachelor cohabitation with Holmes. The *premise* of the series, almost sit-com like, depends on Holmes and Watson sharing rooms, with Mrs Hudson making breakfasts and clients appearing weekly, and Doyle understood he had been too hasty in having his characters move on. This is a typical example of an author not knowing as he is writing how his series will develop, establishing things which later need to be revoked or ignored — most blatantly, Holmes's death in 'The Final Problem'.

Of course, the lapses and lacunae are useful for subsequent hands.

S*herlock Holmes: The Hidden Years*, edited by Michael Kurland, is the latest of many collections of Holmes stories from authors not Sir Arthur Conan Doyle. It deals with 'the great hiatus', that period between 'The Final Problem' and 'The Empty House' (which happens to be between the first and second Klinger volumes) when Holmes was thought dead by all the world and away from London on mysterious adventures. What actually happened was this: Doyle decided to kill Holmes and delivered an entirely satisfying finale, bringing on a suitable arch-nemesis in Professor Moriarty and having the antagonists perish in a plunge over the Reichenbach Falls, with just enough ambiguity (the bodies are never found) to provide a get-out clause or the possibility that Holmes, like King Arthur, sleeps somewhere until England has direst need of him. As soon as the detective was dead, readers, editors and publishers were clamouring for his resurrection, and eventually Doyle caved in and — as is often forgotten — turned out *The Hound of the Baskervilles*, the most famous and best-liked of the novels, establishing that it takes place before 'The Final Problem'. There was no real reason that this approach shouldn't have been continued (almost all the stories published after *Baskervilles*, well into the 1920s, are set in the late Victorian/early Edwardian era), but an *actual* return from the dead was demanded and paid for. Doyle duly delivered 'The Empty House', which has to squirm mightily to give an explanation not only for Holmes's survival but for his absence and (in retrospect) cruel deception of his closest friend.

As Kurland, author of some excellent novels with Moriarty as the lead, points out in his introduction, the explanation in 'The

Empty House' won't do. It was the best Doyle could manage, and the *story* is rather a good one, but by this time the pleasures of the Holmes canon were less to do with the plot business than with the central characters and their relationship. Readers can believe in the dastardliness of Colonel Moran and all the narrative elements are sound, but Holmes's treatment of Watson doesn't square with the character we thought we knew — which is why some have said the post-Reichenbach Holmes is someone else or a fiction (this is an instance of the ingratitude cited above — ascribing all the *vintage* Holmes tales to Watson, but blaming Doyle for the lesser stuff). A few of Kurland's contributors, following Nicholas Meyer in *The Seven-per-cent-Solution*, simply put it out that 'The Final Problem' and 'The Empty House' are not 100% accurate and set out stories that explain why this is so: Gary Lovisi's 'The Adventure of the Missing Detective' has Holmes take a trip to a parallel world where Moriarty has triumphed and brought about a dystopia by assassinating Queen Victoria and all that travelling-in-Tibet-disguised-as-a-Norwegian business is a cover for a tale that wouldn't have been believed, while Kurland himself in 'Reichenbach' has the whole death-and-return business a deception on the part of Holmes and Moriarty who are actually reluctant allies on a secret mission for Mycroft.

Others set the veracity or otherwise of Holmes's account to one side and tell stories that *don't* contradict the originals. Michael Mallory's 'The Beast of Guangming Peak' and Carolyn Wheat's 'Water From the Moon' — like Jamyang Norbu's fine novel *The Mandala of Sherlock Holmes* — look exactly to where Holmes says he was (the Himalayas), and spin mysteries involving the abominable snowman and the Great Game of imperial espionage (no one goes for North Africa, where Holmes also says he was). Linda Robertson's 'The Mystery of Dr Thorvald Sigerson', Michael Collins' 'Cross of Gold', Carole Buggé's 'The Strange Case of the Voodoo Priestess' and Bill Pronzini's 'The Bughouse Caper' have Holmes spend time in America (which Holmes doesn't mention in 'The Empty House'), presumably because they are Americans and know the territory best. These stories all tie Holmes in with traditions of American detection: Collins works a connection with his own Dan Fortune series (and discerns a socially-committed, left-leaning Holmes), Buggé and Pronzini partner Holmes with San Francisco and New Orleans dicks (one a sceptical hardboiled PI, the other an impressed scientific policeman) and Robertson has Holmes-Sigerson solve an elementary puzzle in an interesting locale (Alaska).

The most interesting, if not necessarily the finest, stories take advantage of the hiatus to give us a Holmes through eyes other than those of the hero-worshipping and perhaps naïve Dr Watson. Rhys Bowen's 'The Case of the Lugubrious Manservant' has Freud treat an amnesiac who turns out to be a post-Fall Holmes and gives this away in its subtitle (how much more interesting if it had been Moriarty?) and provides a *third* Freudian analysis of the detective (after novels by Meyer and Keith Oates). Peter Beagle's 'Mr. Sigerson' (which *is* the finest story here) has Holmes working as a violinist in a mittel European orchestra in an adventure recounted by a more sceptical narrator who doesn't much care for the detective, presenting a mystery of the sort Doyle liked along with an emotional tangle which might have been beyond his range. This is an instance of a pastiche with a point, as much a criticism as a celebration not only of Holmes but of Doyle; almost all the other stories are fun — even indulgent fun like Richard Lupoff's pulp-reference-packed 'God of the Naked Unicorn' — and one or two provide some plot or character meat, but Beagle probes the deepest and hits a nerve. ✗

Kim Newman is a novelist (Anno Dracula, Life's Lottery) *and critic* (Nightmare Movies, Apocalypse Movies). *His latest books are* Horror: Another 100 Best Books *(co-edited with Stephen Jones) and the short story collection* Dead Travel Fast. *Forthcoming are another collection,* The Man From the Diogenes Club, *and a study of the UK TV series* Doctor Who. *He is also working on a BBC-TV documentary about Sherlock Holmes,* A Study in Sherlock.

SCREEN OF THE CRIME

by Lenny Picker

- The Curious Incident of the Hound in the Night-time, or, Why *The Hound of the Baskervilles* is unfilmable

THE CURSE OF THE HOUND —

There have been many movie and television adaptations of *The Hound of the Baskervilles,* yet, as I come to my computer screen in a direct line from repeated marathon viewings of eight of the nine most recent serious versions, I am setting down some thoughts and observations as to why, for this longtime Holmesian at least, none have come close to capturing the essence of the best-known and most popular Sherlock Holmes story, which pits the ultimate rationalist against a supernatural legend. I have been grappling with the challenge *The Hound* poses for filmmakers for over fifteen years; as an admirer of Granada Television's series starring Jeremy Brett, I was stunned at how inadequate Granada's adaptation was and began to wonder why it was a failure. (That view, by the way, is one that was shared by one of the preeminent authorities on that version — as will be discussed below.) That led me to analyze the original story itself, and to undertake a close study of the problems it has presented to other media, film in particular. I will touch on the 1939 (Rathbone), 1959 (Cushing), 1968 (Cushing), 1972 (Granger), 1983 (Richardson), 1988 (Brett), 2001 (Frewer) and 2002 (Roxburgh) versions; as a copy of the 1982 BBC production starring Tom Baker has eluded me, I have not relied on my twenty-three-year-old memories of it for this column. In this column, I will try to identify those challenges, to look at how various directors and screenwriters have tried to meet them, and to suggest possible approaches for the next brave and foolhardy souls to take a crack at bringing *The Hound* to life.

[SPOILER ALERT: Those who have not yet read *The Hound of the Baskervilles*, please be warned that the novel's secrets are revealed below. —MK]

THE BOOK —

The plot of *The Hound* is doubtless familiar to all readers of this magazine, but a brief synopsis may be useful for the discussion to follow. Holmes is consulted by Dr Mortimer, who recounts a seventeenth-century legend of a curse plaguing the aristocratic Baskerville family of Dartmoor, ever since a decadent family member fell victim to the jaws of a demonic hound. Mortimer proceeds to describe the recent mysterious death of Sir Charles Baskerville, who was found with his features horribly distorted, as if he had died of sheer terror, and in proximity to traces of the fabled monstrous dog. Mortimer, fearing for the life of Sir Henry Baskerville, the successor to the estate, seeks Holmes's guidance. When the heir, undeterred by a warning letter, the theft of two boots, and a sinister shadow, decides to inhabit Baskerville Hall, Watson is assigned to accompany him, both as a bodyguard and on-the-scene investigator. He diligently reports his observations and speculations to Holmes, stuck in London on another case. Watson meets the neighbors — the naturalist Stapleton and his attractive sister Beryl, and Frankland, a local litigious crank estranged from his daughter. Watson himself hears a "long, low moan," which Stapleton identifies as the sound the local peasants attribute to the hound of the Baskervilles. Sir Henry rapidly falls in love with Beryl. Suspicious nocturnal ramblings by the Baskerville butler, Barrymore, first suggest his involvement in the plot against the family he has served, but the good doctor and Sir Henry discover that the servant has been providing supplies to his brother-in-law, Selden, a murderous escaped convict in hiding on the moor. Their pursuit of Selden is unsuccessful, but during it, Watson spots a mysterious figure outlined against the moonlight. When Sir Henry agrees to keep Selden's whereabouts a secret until he can leave the country, Barrymore shares a clue suggesting that a woman had lured Sir Charles to his fatal appointment. Watson not only traces the woman, Laura Lyons, but tracks down the mysterious figure, who is revealed as Holmes himself. To keep his investigations free from scrutiny, the detective had been hiding on the moor himself, putting together clues that led him to label Sir Charles' death a murder, and Stapleton as the culprit. But, as proof of the scientist's guilt is lacking, Holmes plots to catch him red-handed, a strategy that seems to fail when the hound claims another victim. This time, Selden, who had been wearing the baronet's cast-off clothing, is the victim. To lure Stapleton into a trap, Holmes and

Watson pretend to return to London; instead, they lie in wait as Stapleton sets his beast on Sir Henry, fatally shooting the animal just in the nick of time. The creature is revealed to be a huge ferocious dog, daubed with phosphorous to create a supernatural aura; its master, in reality Sir Henry's cousin with eyes on the succession, who had forced his wife to pose as his sister to tempt his relative, flees into the mire, and is apparently sucked into its depths.

Of course, such a Monarch Notes-like summary cannot begin to conjure up the incredible experience of reading the book itself. Sir Arthur Conan Doyle wrote it as a way to sate the public's demand for more Holmes, without bringing Holmes back permanently, so he set *The Hound* before the fateful Reichenbach Falls death-struggle with the Napoleon of Crime; yet it is not only one of his best stories, *The Hound* is unquestionably one of the great Gothic mysteries of all time, if not the greatest: replete with memorable lines ("Mr. Holmes, they were the footprints of a gigantic hound!", "forbear from crossing the moor in those dark hours when the powers of evil are exalted.") and unforgettable scenes — especially Chapter 14's climactic appearance of "the dreadful shape which had sprung out upon us from the fog." Watson's reports to Holmes from Baskerville Hall vividly create a mood of dread and suspense that most others authors labor at in vain. While locked-room aficionados can legitimately debate which John Dickson Carr puzzle is the trickiest impossible crime yarn ever, no rivals to *The Hound* immediately spring to mind (a quick challenge to the reader — name one without thinking for a few minutes).

FILMING THE STORY —

For many readers, it is only natural to seek to extend the pleasures of a favorite book by experiencing the story in a different medium such as film. And in some cases, movies have actually improved upon the original, preserving the original structure while altering minor plot details to make the story more logical or more resonant. (For example, the Peter Ustinov version of Agatha Christie's *Death on the Nile*, which was far superior to the overly-faithful and listless recent David Suchet version).

Ironically, because *The Hound* is so well-loved, translating it to film is harder than adapting a lesser-known story — as Bert Coules, the supremely-gifted head writer on the BBC's recent radio dramatization of the complete Canon, has observed, "Because people love the best known stories — *The Hound of the Baskervilles*, 'The Speckled Band,' — they have very fixed ideas about what can and cannot be done with them." But "harder" is not the same as "impossible." A few years ago, many devoted Tolkien fans would have been skeptical that any film adaptation of *The Lord of the Rings* could do that master work of romantic fantasy justice, and yet, in the loving hands of Peter Jackson, three superb films were made that have not only brought Tolkien's epic to a wider audience, but satisfied many of his most devoted fans. So what is it about *The Hound* that has been so difficult to master?

Space limitations preclude a more-detailed critique of each film, or an enumeration of the gratuitous and often odd changes to the story. For example, the impact of the 1939 Dr Mortimer's account of his observations of traces upon the ground was somewhat dissipated because it came *before* the legend was recounted, making the presence of a pawprint ominous, not merely odd.

DOGS THAT DON'T HUNT —

It should go without saying that any film version of *The Hound* that does not scare, startle, or give viewers the creeps has not done its duty; the original story is more of an eerie thriller than a study in ratiocination. And yet none of the film versions have evoked such feelings in me. A large part of the answer lies in the immense difficulty, if not impossibility, of matching the drama of the book by creating "an enormous coal-black hound, but not such a hound as mortal eyes have ever seen." The images our individual imaginations have conjured of the creature, with "[f]ire burst[ing] from its open mouth, its eyes glow[ing] with a smouldering glare, its muzzle and hackles and dewlap . . . outlined in flickering flame" may never be satisfied by another's vision. I will not spend time here comparing the dogs who have been miscast, or, as in the latest BBC version, mis-computer-generated, in the story's title role — suffice to say that none have struck me as being scary, and some (especially the 1959 animal, "enhanced" with a rabbit-skin mask) have been unintentionally silly-looking.

But many versions also make the mistake of showing their hand (or paw, as it were) too early, leaving little doubt from the outset that a flesh-and-blood dog is involved. The 1983 Ian Richardson version, for example, has a long opening scene of a dapper Sir Charles awaiting a visitor *inside* a summer-house actually connected to Baskerville Hall itself, before a ferocious black dog breaks through the glass doors and attacks him (magically leaving no marks on the body.) The makers of 2001's *The Hound* with Matt Frewer have their canine appear in broad daylight, at one point staring up at Sir Henry as he looks out of his ancestral home towards the moor. Even the 1939 Basil Rathbone vehicle shows a dog pushing Selden to his death. These explicit depictions lessen the force of the story's climax — we have seen the hellhound several times before the attack on Sir Henry, and so there is less for us to be startled by.

Pacing is another basic component to a tale of suspense. The comatose pace of the Granada production was perhaps its biggest shortcoming. As noted above, my dim view of the 1988 Granada production is not idiosyncratic. In David Stuart Davies's comprehensive *Starring Sherlock Holmes*, the author cites a conversation he had with Jeremy Brett not long before the actor's untimely passing. When Davies asked Brett "if he could have a final crack at one of the unfilmed Holmes stories, which would it be? Without hesitation he replied, 'I'd like to do *The Hound* again. I think we can do much better than that. I was terribly unwell making the film. It was underconceived. The script drifted — which is fatal. Holmes was away too long."

And although a *Hound*-like plot, complete with a glowing marsh monster, was employed to great effect in Rathbone's later, non-period *The Scarlet Claw*, his *Hound*, with a surprising lack of mood music, often failed to grip. By contrast, one of the areas in which the 2002 Roxburgh *Hound* succeeded was in its dramatic, pulse-pounding, and very different opening, with the inquest into Sir Charles' death punctuated with flashbacks to his autopsy.

None of these would seem to be insurmountable obstacles. CGI technology that can create a plausible Gollum should be able to create an animal that matches Doyle's words. (According to Sherlockian film expert Phil Cornell, in a recent issue of the scion publication, *The Passenger's Log*, there was some talk in the late 1970s of Peter Cushing appearing in his third version of *The Hound*, which would have featured a stop-frame animation hellhound from special effects master Ray Harryhausen.) And a subtle hand could content itself with terrifying off-screen howls, suggestive silhouettes, or other tried-and-true tricks of the trade to ratchet up the suspense, even among those members of the audience who can recite the text of Watson's second report from Baskerville Hall verbatim.

HOLMES AWAY FROM HOLMES —

Perhaps as equal a difficulty for the screenwriter is to stay true to the spirit of the book while finely adjusting the storyline so that there is more Holmes. *The Hound* is the only one of the long stories without a lengthy back-story set in India or America, but it still goes for a fairly long stretch without Holmes' presence. "This works really well in a book, as we associate with Watson on his own, for after all he is our story-teller, he holds the point-of-view. But in a film that is not the case, and the audience feels dislocated not to be with Holmes," observes David Pirie, author of *The Dark Water,* the only recent pastiche that succeeds in pitting a Holmesian sleuth against an evil that may be otherworldly.

The 1973 *Hound* with Stewart Granger expands Holmes's role by having him initially accompany Sir Henry, Mortimer and Watson to Dartmoor, before concocting an excuse that will enable him to continue his inquiries in secret. In theory, such a liberty could work, but given the poor casting and production values of that effort, it is not so easy to visualize that plot alteration in a better-quality adaptation. Perhaps someone with imagination could craft an early Holmes-Stapleton encounter that would prove to reveal an important clue.

At the other extreme is the 2001 Matt Frewer production, although many may feel that the decision not to have his quirky, self-parodying Holmes reveal himself on Dartmoor until he shucks off a disguise and takes potshots at a blinded hound that hunts by smell alone to have been a wise choice under the circumstances. The lack of intelligence in that version's script is demonstrated by its inclusion of a scene in which Kenneth Welsh's very able (if elderly) Watson tracks down Holmes's lair in the stone hut, without actually tracking down Holmes himself.

Other productions, most notably the 2002 BBC version, tack on lengthy invented scenes to play up the Holmes-Stapleton battle of wits, seeking to elevate the secret Baskerville to Moriarty-like dimensions of villainy. Once again, with the right cast, and writing faithful in spirit to the Canon, such scenes could address the problem of the missing Holmes, but the efforts thus far have sacrificed fidelity to the story's spirit for action or postmodern recursions (when Richard Roxburgh's Holmes insists that Stapleton's schemes will leave little mark on the world, his adversary knowingly counters that he will achieve immortality because of the fame of Holmes himself, a conceit that just doesn't work).

One option that has not been attempted comes from Denis O. Smith, the brilliant author of some of the best pastiches ever written, including "The Secret of Shoreswood Hall," one of the very few tales to capture the spirit of *The Hound,* and who richly deserves to be widely read both within Sherlockian circles and the general mystery-loving public. He has suggested that a screenwriter could give Holmes more actual detective work to do while on Dartmoor than would actually be shown; perhaps more grilling of Dr Mortimer and/or Stapleton about the ancient legend that could expose questions about its provenance (after all, as commentators have long pointed out, the text says nothing about how Sir Charles's predecessor met his end, and if he did not die in a manner consistent with the legend, why would Sir Charles have taken it so seriously?)

THE ACTOR PLAYING SIR HUGO DUNIT —

Many mystery readers don't focus on the fact that, as Bert Coules puts it, "Most of Doyle's stories are not detective stories in the modern sense of the word." The solutions in the Canon are often either not particularly surprising, or not based on fair-play clues carefully sprinkled beforehand. In some ways, *The Hound* is more of a mystery than many others of the original sixty. Denis Smith has commented that *The Hound* "is also notable for being one of the very few of Doyle's stories which is presented pretty much in the form which was to become popular later in the 1920s and '30s, that is, an initial mystery plus a cast of innocent-seeming, if somewhat eccentric local characters, one of whom, you suspect, may in fact be the villain. It is also almost unique among Doyle's Holmes stories in having a sub-plot (the business with Selden and the Barrymores) which is dragged across the path of the main plot like a red herring, to confuse the issue."

Even so, Doyle unveils the man behind the dog earlier on in the book than might be deemed ideal. (Bert Coules, again — Doyle "gives away the identity of the murderer quite incidentally. It's almost thrown away, a long way before the end of the story.") And some film versions give the show away even earlier than that by casting the same actors (1972's William Shatner and 1983's Nicholas Clay) as both Sir Hugo and Stapleton without taking any pains to make the family resemblance a subtle one. Others (the 1988 Granada for one) show too much of the mysterious figure dogging Sir Henry in London to make his identity much of a mystery.

Suspense concerning the hand on the devil-dog's leash could be enhanced by delaying the revelation of the villain's identity (although Basil Rathbone in 1939 only risked his client's life a second time by not sharing his suspicions with Watson until the very end of the film), or, as Denis Smith suggests, by writing in "in a few extra encounters with Frankland and Mortimer, to try to make them appear a little furtive or suspicious, and possibly making a little more of Laura Lyons's absconding husband." Efforts along these lines have been attempted — the 1939 and 1959 versions do make token efforts to transform the genial young Mortimer of the book into a scowling, belligerent figure with some secrets to hide, but fail to develop the concept. (Many Holmesian scholars have noted plot inconsistencies in the original — how did the doctor's spaniel make its way to the heart of the Grimpen

Mire? — that suggest to them that Mortimer and Stapleton were in league. And the first Cushing *Hound* featured a half-hearted attempt to cast suspicion on Frankland, now both an entomologist and a bishop, by introducing a deadly spider into the action. The 1983 Richardson adaptation substitutes a brutal drunkard Geoffrey Lyons, complete with Roylott-like poker-bending strength, for Frankland, but then undercuts the logic of the plot by not only having his wife strangled, thus eliminating any residual belief that unearthly forces might have been at work in Sir Charles' death, but by showing Lyons snoring downstairs while she is murdered., thus eliminating him as a suspect. Having Laura Lyons killed by Stapleton — but in a way that suggests she fell afoul of the legendary hound — could be a logical amplification of Doyle's story — after all, the original text has Holmes remarking that she had had a "fortunate escape," having had Stapleton in her power.

UNPLUMBED DEPTHS —

There are abundant variations on the basic plot that could give a film version a better shot at creating menace, fear and suspense. The supernatural angle could be played up. Intriguingly, one of the few (if not the only) interesting aspects of the Granger *Hound* is its very ending, when a mournful howl echoes over the moors *after* Stapleton and his beast have sunk into the Grimpen Mire, suggesting that the curse has not ended after all . . .

A similar notion was to be the basis of an unmade Keith McConnell Holmes film, *The Werewolf of the Baskervilles*, which reportedly postulated that the family had been haunted by a lycanthrope all along. Incorporating aspects of the various myths that may have been the "west county legend"Fletcher Robinson recounted to Doyle also could provide new angles that could help. (The Roxburgh Hound does portray the beast of the legend as a loyal pet defending his mistress's honour, rather than an instrument of satanic forces, but does virtually nothing with this innovation.) Given Holmes' encyclopedic knowledge, it would not be surprising that a man who kept entries in his commonplace book for vampires would be aware of the Whist Hounds or the Black Dog of Dartmoor, and be able to employ that knowledge to uncover Stapleton's scheme.

A NEW HOPE? —

Perhaps, despite the pessimism of this column's subtitle, *The Hound* is not an unscalable peak. When analyzed, flaw by flaw, the problems with these films should be susceptible to correction. Perhaps we, as the second Hugo Baskerville might have put it, (if he were alive today, and a reader of *SHMM*), should learn then from this essay not to fear the fruits of these past adaptations, but rather put to use them as a prism to highlight Doyle's original remarkable act of creation. And when the next version hits the screen, just maybe it will be the product of a Sherlockian Peter Jackson, who could be out there, even as I write, preparing a film that deserves Doyle's own description of his work, a film that is "a real Creeper." ✗

Leonard Picker, an inspector general in New York City, has written on the Master for Publishers Weekly, Alfred Hitchcock's Mystery Magazine, *and the* Baker Street Miscellanea, *and is fortunate to be married to someone willing to sit through six straight hours of Hound movies without complaint. He may be contacted at chthompson@jtsa.edu.*

ASK MRS HUDSON

by (Mrs) Martha Hudson

It is both gratifying and a tad onerous that ever since I became landlady to the illustrious Mr. Sherlock Holmes, my life has become richly endowed with incident, and at times is downright adventurous. One may therefore well imagine the enlarged experience that such an association brings an industrious gentlewoman as I hope I may represent myself.

Mr. Holmes's dear friend Dr John H. Watson has encouraged me to share this store of worldly knowledge with the readers of this apposite periodical. To get things started, he has solicited several queries which I have endeavoured to answer below.

In future, should you wish to seek my advice, address your query to Ask Mrs Hudson at <mrshudson@wildsidepress.com>. Letters may be of a personal or impersonal nature; I am happy to give advice on any topic whatsoever.

Sincerely,

(Mrs) MARTHA HUDSON

✗   ✗   ✗

Dear Mrs Hudson,

I am an American, and my cousin is almost forty, lives alone, is meticulous to a fault (I once caught him refolding the guest towels after I had used the lavatory). He shies away from women — in fact, he seems afraid of them. He is a member of the Guilford Choral Society, and enjoys Gilbert and Sullivan operettas. He says his years at a boys' public school were the best of his life, even though I know the boys were beaten and forced to take cold showers. Is he "peculiar?"

Sincerely,

Puzzled in Pembroke

Dear Puzzled,

Don't worry about your cousin. No, he is not peculiar; he is merely British.

Yours,

Mrs Hudson

✗   ✗   ✗

Dear Mrs Hudson,

My mother in law goes everywhere with us — holidays, shopping trips, even restaurants. To make matters worse, she lives next door and has taken to popping over for tea without being in-

vited. She goes on at length regarding my performance as a wife and housekeeper — I wasn't even allowed to buy drapes for the bedroom without her advice. When I complain to my husband, he says he only wants to be a good son and that I should be more respectful of my elders.
Ignored in Ipswich

Dear Ignored:
Here is what you should do: Have your husband transfer his assets to your name, then book a one-way ticket for one to Palermo. Take a train in the middle of the night. Leave no forwarding address. Get an Italian boyfriend. He will be just as attached to his mother, but it will be worth it, as he will be much better in bed.
Ciao,
Mrs Hudson

✗   ✗   ✗

Dear Mrs Hudson,
My husband likes to dress in women's clothing. Should I divorce him?
Doubtful in Dublin

Dear Doubtful,
Not unless he looks better than you do in heels.
Sincerely,
Mrs Hudson

✗   ✗   ✗

Dear Mrs Hudson,
My Labrador retriever Wellington has taken to sleeping in the bed next to me. He's become so bossy about it, in fact, that my poor husband has to sleep on the couch these days. In fact, if poor Jacques tries to come anywhere near the bed, Wellie growls and snaps at him. What should I do about this?
Snoozing in Sussex

Dear Snoozing,
Yes, you certainly are. What on earth do you expect when you name a dog after a general who famously defeated Napoleon? Your dog is merely living up to his namesake by re-enacting the battle between England and France, attacking your poor husband, who has the misfortune to have a French name. Your husband may not be much of a man (as I strongly suspect, as he is allowing a Labrador retriever to intimidate him), but he deserves his place beside you in bed. Give away the dog, if you must, but restore your poor beleaguered Jacques to his rightful place before he loses all of his self respect. And for god's sake, tell

the new owners to give the dog a new name!
    Votre servante,
        Mrs Hudson

✗   ✗   ✗

Dear Mrs Hudson,
    I am frightfully sorry to bother you, but you see, my girl went and ran with my old school chum, Charlie. Not that he's a bad sort, mind you; he's a regular decent chap, I suppose; a bit of a prankster on the old rugby pitch, you know — he's just a little fellow, don't you know, so he played scrum half, only he wasn't that keen on it — rugger, I mean, so he was always a bit bulloxed. Good fun, really, at the parties afterward. Always had something amusing on his head — lampshades, a plate of salmon mouse, the fullback's underwear. But I mean, sod it — what a rotter, to go and do something like that! I mean, it does really take a bit of cheek, doesn't it, to go and pinch a fellow's girl? The thing is, you see, I'd like to show I'm a good sport and all that by getting them a nice wedding present. Any suggestions?
    Stranded in Surrey

Dear Stranded,
    Have you considered cyanide? I believe there's a sale on just now at Harrods. And for god's sake, you sound like an upper class ponce. Try talking like a sensible, normal person and maybe your next lady friend won't leave you for a scrum half.
    Cheerio,
        Mrs Hudson

✗   ✗   ✗

Dear Mrs Hudson,
    Do onions store well in a root cellar over the winter?
        Wondering in Woolwich

Dear Wondering,
    Yes, they do. I am including my recipe for onion and wild mushroom tart, which is a great favourite of Mr Holmes and Dr Watson. Wild mushrooms are best, but store bought ones will do
    Sincerely,
        Mrs Hudson

✗   ✗   ✗

MRS HUDSON'S WILD MUSHROOM TART

Pastry dough
1 tablespoon unsalted butter
1 tablespoon vegetable oil

3/4 lb mixed fresh wild mushrooms such as morels,
    oyster, and chanterelle, quartered lengthwise
2 tablespoons finely chopped shallot
1/2 cup finely chopped onion
1 teaspoon chopped fresh thyme
1 tablespoon fresh parsley
3/4 teaspoon salt
3/8 teaspoon black pepper
1/2 cup crème fraîche
1/2 cup heavy cream
1 whole large egg
1 large egg yolk

Special equipment: a 9- by 1-inch round fluted tart pan with a removable bottom; pie weights or raw rice

Make shell:

Roll out dough on a lightly floured surface with a lightly floured rolling pin into an 11-inch round and fit into tart pan, trimming excess dough. Chill until firm, about 30 minutes.

Put oven rack in middle position and preheat oven to 375°F.

Lightly prick bottom of shell all over with a fork, then line with foil and fill with pie weights. Bake until side is set and edge is pale golden, 18 to 20 minutes. Carefully remove foil and weights and bake shell until bottom is golden, 10 to 15 minutes more.

Cool completely in pan on a rack, about 15 minutes.

Make filling while shell bakes:

Heat butter and oil in a 12-inch heavy skillet over moderately high heat until foam subsides, then sauté mushrooms, shallot, onion, thyme, parsley, 1/2 teaspoon salt, and 1/4 teaspoon pepper, stirring frequently, until mushrooms are tender and any liquid given off is evaporated, 8 to 10 minutes. Transfer to a bowl and cool to room temperature.

Whisk together crème fraîche, heavy cream, whole egg, yolk, and remaining 1/4 teaspoon salt and 1/8 teaspoon pepper in a medium bowl until combined.

Fill and bake tart:

Reduce oven temperature to 325°F.

Scatter mushrooms evenly in tart shell and pour custard over them. Bake tart in pan on a baking sheet until custard is just set and slightly puffed, 35 to 45 minutes.

Cool tart in pan on rack at least 20 minutes, then remove side of pan. Serve tart warm or at room temperature.   ✗

SHMM SPEAKS WITH RON GOULART

Interview conducted by Carole Buggé

Ron Goulart is one of the most prolific genre authors with more than 180 published works, including approximately fifty science fantasy novels and twenty mystery novels, including his popular series starring Groucho Marx as detective. His Harry Challenge stories are special favorites of this magazine's editor, who has commissioned several new stories in the series. Twice nominated for the Mystery Writers of America's Edgar award, Ron Goulart is an acknowledged expert on comic books and pulp magazines; his most recent book, just published, is *Cheap Thrills, an Informal History of the Pulp Magazines*. He and his wife Frances, who is also a writer, live in Ridgefield, Connecticut.

SHMM: Where were you born?

Ron Goulart: In Berkeley, California. That was in January of 1933, just a couple of months before Roosevelt was inaugurated for the first of several terms as President. I grew up in a peaceful, pleasant neighborhood, even though it was on the wrong side of the tracks.

SHMM: What did your parents do?

RG: My father came to America from the Azore Islands when he was in his teens and worked in the same factory for the next fifty years. He was a dapper, handsome fellow in his youth and in Oakland, where he then resided, his friends called him the Sheik of Kirkham Street. My mother, who was born in this country, grew up in Oakland with a bunch of siblings and a one-armed father. She worked in a couple of factories, one of which manufactured light bulbs, until she married. In the early 1940's, she started working as the head cook in the cafeteria of the Berkeley grammar school that I attended. She stayed at that job until she died of cancer at the age of forty-five. I'm an only child, as is my wife. Makes for very sparsely attended family reunions.

SHMM: What in your background led to a writing career?

RG: Writing was only one of several careers I had my eye on as a kid. Our family consumed all the cheap popular arts forms — movies, radio, pulp magazines, library books and (for me, anyway) funny papers and comic books. I saw no reason why I couldn't grow up to be a writer, a star of stage, screen and radio, a comedian and a cartoonist who drew a newspaper strip and a batch of comic books. From grade school through college I fooled with all of these callings. Wrote and drew for the high school newspaper, wrote and drew for the college humor magazine (at UC Berkeley), starred in the senior play at high school, belonged to a radio workshop that broadcast a dramatic show once a week on a local station, did a standup comedy act that wowed them at Cub Scout picnics and, later, at the Junior Prom.

SHMM: Were your ambitions nurtured by your upbringing and background, or did you have to overcome obstacles?

RG: Neither of my parents wanted me to end up in a factory. So they always encouraged my efforts to aim higher. My mother was convinced that I was destined for greatness and saw to it that by the time I was thirteen I had my own typewriter and drawing board. My father, more practical, suggested that I also think about an occupation to fall back on. That's why I told the folks at UC that I wanted to become an English teacher.

SHMM: When did you get started writing?

RG: I was telling stories at school show-and-tell days from the first grade on and putting them on paper from about the second. I started submitting stories to professional magazines from the time I was about fifteen. I collected rejection slips from *Planet Stories, Thrilling Wonder, Weird Tales* and *The New Yorker*. When I was about sixteen or thereabouts I signed up for a one-night-a-week writing class that Anthony Boucher taught out of his house up on the right side of the tracks. I was certain that once he saw a sample of my work, I'd become a regular contributor to his *Magazine of Fantasy & Science Fiction*. It didn't work out that way and I was nineteen before I made my first sale to *F&SF*.

SHMM: Did you ever have to support yourself with "day jobs," and if so, what were they and what were they like? Did any of them feed your writing?

RG: I've always, once I got out of college, supported myself by writing. However, for the first dozen or so years I wrote copy for ad agencies in addition to selling stories to *F&SF, Amazing, Hitchcock,* etc. What I'd do was work for a couple of years at an agency, then quit and live on my savings while writing stories. The first year I tried this I wrote fifty stories, sent out about twenty-five and sold six. When my money ran out I'd go back into the ad game for a couple more years. I was a pretty good copywriter, and also fast, so I didn't have much trouble getting a job. The San Francisco agency where I did two stretches hired me initially after reading some of what I'd written for the college humor magazine. That saved me from a life of teaching, as well as kept me from living off a generous pension now.

SHMM: Which of your books or stories do you like most, and why?

RG: I like most everything I've written over the years. Right now the Groucho Marx mystery novels I'm doing for St. Martin's Press strike me as being pretty good — and funny. The latest one, Groucho Marx, King of the Jungle, is about a murder on the set of a Tarzan-like movie. It'll be appearing in a book store near you this July. And I've always been fond of Harry Challenge in both novels and short stories.

SHMM: With regard to comic books, what have you done, and what your views of the genre's significance? When did your interest in comics begin, and what are some of your likes and dislikes?

RG: I got hooked on funnies at a very early age. I was reading the Sunday comic sections before I could read, spreading them out on the kitchen floor and savoring the pictures. Comic books came along about the same time I did, and I started buying them (financed by my mother) from about the age of four. Graphic images of all sorts have always appealed to me, even the ones I turn out. In the middle 1970's, Gil Kane and his family moved into the same Connecticut town where we were living. He was a great fan of science fiction and was familiar with my work. Or so he said. He introduced me to Roy Thomas, who was the head editor at Marvel back then. I got about a dozen scripting jobs, mostly adaptations of H.P. Lovecraft, Robert Bloch and the like. In the late 1970's, Kane and I collaborated on a syndicated comic strip called Star Hawks. In the 1990's I wrote the first eighteen issues of William Shatner's Tekworld for Marvel. I was never able to work on DC comic books and the late Julie Schwartz once told me I ought to stick to novel writing. I still buy comic books every week and like a wide range of stuff, from Bone to 100 Bullets.

SHMM: Which genre authors influenced your style and career?

RG: I wrote fan letters to a few of my favorite writers in my distant youth: Edgar Rice Burroughs, Sax Rohmer and Leslie

Charteris among them. Burroughs and Rohmer obliged with autographs and a few kind words. Charteris actually wrote a couple of letters answering my questions. I read Charteris in those days not for his plots but for the adventure and the humor. The Saint was all over the place in the 1940's. Movies, radio, comics and the affordable two-bit paperback. Charteris even had his own paperback outfit — Chartered Books for a time. The lesson from him was that a mystery could also be funny. It wasn't until years later that I learned that some of his stuff was ghosted. By Henry Kutter (another of my favorites), Cleve Cartmill, etc.

SHMM: Do you have advice or observations on the plotting process, which some writers regard as the toughest part of story writing?

RG: My approach to plotting? My basic theory is that a good short story is constructed like a good joke. Or maybe a good shaggy dog story. So you have to know the punchline before you can start telling it. Usually I try to know what the ending is going to be and sometimes I even write out the last lines first. That way, I know where I'm heading. I must admit that in recent years I sometimes start a story without that punchline clearly in mind. To get myself going on the plotting process, I often think up titles first. Those often trigger a plot. Although I have some titles that I jotted down years ago and am still trying to figure out a story to go with. One a long time on my list is *The Case of the Extra Ventriloquist.* Another method for me to get a plot going is to put the end at the beginning, but in a vague way that is hopefully intriguing. For example — "As to why they found his body floating in the Pacific wearing those strange shoes." Then you go back and explain why. Another source of inspiration is the old *what if?* approach. Works for both fantasy and mystery.

SHMM: Where do you think the business is going? What's wrong — or right — with it?

RG: No idea. I just hope it lasts as long as I do.

SHMM: This issue contains a new Harry Challenge story. How did you come up with Harry and his magician sidekick in the first place?

RG: Harry was inspired in part by my interest in Victorian fiction. Especially the sort of romantic thrillers produced by the likes of Anthony Hope with such novels as *The Prisoner of Zenda*. And there's a bit of an homage to one of the favorite writers of my teens, the incomparable Sax Rohmer. It occurred to me some years ago that there was no reason why I couldn't turn out stuff like that myself. I see the Harry Challenge yarns as falling somewhere between pastiche and spoof. Harry first appeared a couple of decades ago in a paperback novel titled *The Prisoner of Blackwood Castle.* Most all of my novels, even the ones that aren't officially mysteries, tend to have a mystery plot and so it seemed only logical to make Harry a detective in the tradition of both Nick Carter and Carnacki. The Great Lorenzo, his magician friend, was partially inspired by my interest in stage magic of a century ago, especially the gaudy posters. And I've been using plump, avuncular likeable windbags in my stories since grade school days. The other recurring character in the series is Jennie Barr, the daredevil reporter who frequently crosses Harry's path. She's part Nellie Bly, a real life daredevil reporter, and part a fictional reporter that Robert Barr wrote an adventure novel about and part my feisty writer wife.

SHMM: Are there any of your interests outside of your writing that you feel have influenced your writing?

RG: Comics have always been an influence. I've written quite a few stories, as well as a couple of novels, about cartoonists and the comics world. All the radio dramas and comedies I listened to while young also had their effect and I think my habit of telling quite a bit of a story in dialogue I owe to my long ago listening habits. I've always been a fan of jazz and the blues and I've used lines from blues songs for story and book titles — such as *Broke Down Engine.* This is something I was more inclined to do in my younger days. ✗

THE STRANGE CASE OF THE HAUNTED FREIGHTER

by Carole Buggé

"**W**atson, I do believe we have a client."

I looked up from my armchair by the fire at Holmes, who was standing in front of the window, peering down into the street. It was a chilly, overcast day in October, and the grey afternoon light fell listlessly between the parted curtains onto the keen face of my friend, who was as keyed up and attentive as the day was dreary and dull.

"Who might that be, Holmes?" I asked, putting aside the magazine I was reading. His words brought me out of the article I was reading about spiritualism, a subject that my wife had recently become interested in. I myself was more than a little skeptical about the topic, but had agreed to read the article to humour her.

"I can only say that there is every indication that we will have a visitor at any moment."

My wife was in the country visiting her sister, and I had left my surgery in the hands of a colleague for a few days so that Holmes and I could do some ordinance walking in the Lake District. Then we were to meet up with my wife in Windermere, where I was hoping Holmes would take some much needed rest. He had been driving himself too much as usual, having taken on several cases at once. As a result, he had been smoking far too much and eating far too little, and my concern for him had reached such a point that I could no longer hide it. I had suggested the trip to the Lake District not so much for my own sake as for his — I thought that a week of fresh air and exercise might do him some good, stimulate his appetite, and calm his already overstrung nerves.

Now, watching as he stood gazing out the window, my heart sank and I feared that the promised vacation would be indefinitely postponed.

"Look here, Holmes —" I began, but he silenced me with an upheld index finger.

"Yes, Watson, I think that gentleman is definitely in need of our services."

He turned abruptly from the window and flung open the door

to the sitting room.

"Mrs Hudson!" he bellowed out into the hallway. "Could you bring tea for three, please?"

I took the opportunity to go to the window myself and look out, in hopes of seeing whoever it was Holmes had been looking at. The lackluster grey day was surrendering quietly to an early dusk, and visibility outside was poor, but I could just make out a figure in the street below. He was wrapped in a dun colored raincoat with a rubbery sheen to it — the kind of sturdy rain slicker one often saw on professional sailors. He stood next to the stoop of our building, and his stillness set him apart from the forward rush of people hurrying homeward — office workers, umbrellas tucked underneath their arms, the men dressed in bowler hats and gabardine overcoats, the women in long skirts and capes, with short laced ankle boots to protect their feet from the mud and muck of London streets. The man's hat, a wool nautical cap, was pulled low over his eyes, so that I could not see his face.

The rattle of wooden cart wheels, passing merchants' wagons and hansom cabs on the cobblestones accompanied the singsong calls of the street vendors serenading the homeward bound workers, tempting them with their wares:

"Fresh cress, penny a pound!"

"Oy — get yer herring here! Fresh herring!"

"Oysters, cockles, mussels — never better! By them here!"

The mysterious man stood in solitary contrast to the bustle surrounding him. Hands shoved deep into his coat pockets, he leaned up against the building for a few more moments before turning quickly and heading for our front door.

"By Jove, Holmes, I believe you're right," I said as I heard the front doorbell ring. "This fellow has come to see us! How did you know?"

"My dear Watson," Holmes replied, "when a man paces for some time outside of a building, it is a safe bet that he is either waiting for someone or that he is trying to make up his mind whether or not to go inside. In this case, as he did not appear to be waiting for anyone, I could safely surmise that he was intending to pay us a visit, as soon as he collected his wits enough to do so."

"I see. But Holmes, do you think you should be taking on another case just now? I mean, we were planning on getting away."

At that moment Mrs Hudson's short, comfortably plump form appeared at the door. She was carrying a tea tray.

"There's a Mr Crane to see you," she said as she sat the tea upon the table.

"Thank you, Mrs Hudson," Holmes replied. "Would you ask

Mr Crane to come in?"

"It's Captain Crane," said a man's voice behind her.

I turned to see our visitor standing in the doorway. He was tall and lean, with a wiry build similar to Holmes, only broader of shoulder — and his hands had none of the thin nervousness I had come to associate with my friend; they were broad and strong and sunburnt. His face was exceptionally handsome, with luminous, deep-set eyes over high cheekbones and a full mouth. His eyes were a peculiar golden color, like roasted almonds. He wore a dark navy pea jacket, double-breasted with brass buttons, and a simple wool cap, also dark blue, with a leather brim and a yellow braided outline of an anchor on the front. His boots were of good quality, but worn and caked with mud; they looked as though they had not been cleaned in some time.

"Well, Captain Crane, what can I do for you?" Holmes asked.

The captain took a hesitant step into the room. Such timidity sat oddly on a man who was clearly used to giving orders. I wondered what had brought him to our doorstep — he was obviously not the kind of man to seek help lightly.

Holmes turned to Mrs Hudson, who was bustling about setting out the tea. "That will be all, Mrs Hudson, thank you."

The estimable landlady looked as though she wanted to say something, but instead she sighed, turned and departed. I could hear her footsteps as she descended the stairs, favouring her right leg; her knee tended to swell in inclement weather.

"Now then, Captain Crane, won't you join us for tea?" Holmes said. "Or perhaps you'd like something a bit more bracing? A tonic, as it were, against the coming storm?"

The captain took another step into the room and looked around. I had become so inured to Holmes' odd habits that I hardly noticed what must have seemed strange to our visitor — the correspondence attached to the mantelpiece with a pen knife, the chemistry set, the piles of unfiled newspaper clippings stacked in the corners of the room. As Crane gazed around, his hesitancy vanished and was replaced by a firmness of voice and manner, as if he had suddenly made up his mind to the task and was resolved to see it through.

"Very well, Mr Holmes," he replied, "I'll join you for tea, thank you."

"Allow me to introduce my colleague, Dr —"

"Dr Watson, yes," Crane interrupted, seizing my hand in his. His palm was calloused and dry as the skin of a cocoanut. "It is good to meet you," he said, pumping my hand energetically. I felt the athleticism in his powerful grip — I didn't need Holmes to tell me that here was a man accustomed to a vigorous outdoor life.

"My wife introduced me to your writing some years ago," he said, "and I hope you may count me as one of your many admirers."

"Why, thank you," I replied.

"So then, Captain," Holmes interjected, "what takes you away from your ship to seek our advice?"

Holmes was often uncomfortable when it came to any discussion of my writing. I was never sure if that was because of his innate modesty or a buried jealousy he felt toward my accomplishments — or perhaps some combination of both.

"I believe I will take your offer of something stronger, if you don't mind," the captain replied.

"By all means," I answered. "Will cognac do?"

"I'm a plain brandy man, so cognac is a step above my usual fare, thank you."

I went to the sideboard and poured him a stiff cognac. I decided to stick with the tea, as I had a feeling I'd need my wits about me tonight.

"Do have a seat by the fire," Holmes said. "It's a raw night, and I can see that you've been out in it for some time."

"Thank you," our visitor replied, "but I'm used to standing on the bridge in the driving rain on worse nights than this." But he sank wearily into the overstuffed chair next to the fire.

"Yes, I dare say," Holmes remarked, sitting opposite him and pressing his fingers together in the familiar gesture that meant he was studying the man, analyzing him. "You are clearly a man accustomed to taking care of himself — and that is precisely why your case intrigues me. It must be something unsettling indeed that brings you to me."

"Your reputation precedes you, Mr Holmes," the captain replied, taking the snifter of brandy I handed him. His strong hand shook as he raised the glass to his lips. He took a long swallow, letting the liquid slide slowly down his throat. I must admit that I found him a study in contradictions. There was nothing in his manner to suggest the roughness one often found in professional sailors — and his voice was a light and pleasing baritone, more cultivated than what I would have expected from a man of the sea.

"If you don't mind my saying so, Captain," Holmes remarked, "it is plain that you have been going through hard times of late."

"That is true. But how — ?"

"Your clothes are well made, yet there is a button missing from your jacket, and your cuffs are frayed. Your boots are expensive but badly in need of polish — in short, the attire of a man who has troubling things on his mind."

The captain sighed. "What you say is true, Mr Holmes. And your powers of observation which Dr Watson has so often extolled do not disappoint."

Holmes waved off the compliment. "Mere child's play, I assure you. No, apart from the facts I have mentioned, I can tell very little about you. How old were you, by the way, when you contracted scarlet fever as a child? Not more than five, I should think."

The captain sat back in his chair as if he had been pushed.

"Good lord, Mr Holmes! I was just short of my fifth birthday when I came down with the fever. How on earth did you — ?"

"I think I can be of some assistance there," I interjected. "The white spots on your teeth are calcium deposits, likely the result of a high fever as a child, most commonly caused by scarlet fever. Had you been older than five, your teeth would have not been so affected, being beyond the formative stage."

"Excellent, Watson," Holmes said, though I thought I sensed some disappointment in his voice. The magician, having woven the spell, does not like to relinquish the revealing of the trick to an interloper. Nonetheless, Holmes was never less than gracious when I pulled aside the curtain to reveal the mechanics behind the wizardry. "And now, Captain, perhaps we can get to the reason you ventured out on such a foul night."

The captain stared into the firelight and sighed deeply. "Mr Holmes, have you ever lost someone you cared about deeply?"

The question seemed to take Holmes off guard. He swallowed once, then looked away.

"That is neither here nor there, Captain. The point is that you clearly have. That was evident to me the minute you came into the room. And, unless I am mistaken, the loss was rather recent."

The captain nodded. "Yes," he replied in a barely audible whisper. "My wife, Elizabeth . . . gone just three months ago."

"And your visit to me concerns her death in some way."

"Yes."

Holmes stood and studied the rack of pipes upon the mantel. Selecting one made of cherry wood, he plucked the pipe from the rack and turned back to our visitor. "Before you tell me, if you would indulge me for a moment, I'd like to ask just one more question. It may seem to you to be an irrelevant detail, but in my experience it is the details that prove invaluable in the end."

"Yes, of course."

"Then perhaps you would be so kind as to tell me why you recently exchanged your short-haired pointer for a curly-haired spaniel?"

The captain stared at Holmes for a moment, then his face relaxed into a rueful smile.

"By God, Mr Holmes," he murmured, shaking his head, "you *are* a magician. You are correct in what you say — I did recently give Jock away in exchange for my new dog, Bip, who is a Portuguese water dog. "But how did you —"

"Your clothes show evidence of the hair of two different kinds of dog — one has short, whitish hair that you might find on a pointer. Since they are a popular breed just now, and quite at ease around water, I made an educated guess that your previous dog was indeed a pointer."

The captain nodded. "Yes, Jock was a German short-haired pointer, and a good dog at that."

"Indeed. I also observe another kind of hair, which are curly and black and appear to be more recent, as they are not brushed into the fabric of your jacket as were the other hairs. As spaniels are also good water dogs, I ventured a guess as to your current dog."

Crane nodded sadly. "Yes, I regret that I had to give Jock away. You see, he was more my wife's dog than mine, and when she . . . when we lost her, Jock was inconsolable and howled day and night. Poor old fellow . . . I knew how he felt, but finally I just couldn't stand it any more. I found a family outside of Portsmouth who will take good care of him. I wasn't going to get another dog, but Bip turned up on my doorstep one night, shivering and soaking wet, so I kept him. I thought his owner might come looking for him, but they never did. I have to admit he's been a great comfort — he rarely leaves my side. It's almost as though he knows . . ." The captain took a deep breath; I could see him fighting for control of his emotions. "I apologize to both of you," he said finally. "The loss is too recent for me to be entirely in possession of myself."

"Please do not apologize," Holmes replied. "I can see you are a man of deep feeling. Your grief over your wife's death does you credit."

"More brandy?" I suggested, and when he did not object, poured him another stiff one.

"Now, then, Captain, perhaps you could tell us what brings you out on a night like this?" Holmes asked.

Crane paused for a moment and stared into the fire, where the blue-tipped flames licked and twisted around the crackling logs. Then he straightened up in his chair and looked at Holmes. In the firelight his eyes were yellow as wolf's eyes.

"Mr Holmes, have you ever seen a ghost?"

Holmes considered the question carefully before answering.

"I have seen things that cannot be easily explained through use of logic, certainly. Whether or not there is such a thing as 'ghosts' remains to be seen, I think. In the meantime, what do you think?"

The captain took another gulp of brandy, set his glass down, and rose from his chair, as though he could no longer bear to remain still. "I don't know, that's the damnable part of it — I don't know *what* to think!"

"Why don't you start from the beginning?" I suggested gently.

"Yes, yes — I suppose that's the only thing to do. I'll lay the whole thing in front of you and see if you can make any more sense out of it than I have."

I poured him some more brandy and he drank it down without so much as a pause. I could tell he was accustomed to holding his drink — his hands were steadier now. The brandy had warmed him more than the fire, it seemed, and the hesitation in his manner had been replaced by a steadiness in his movements, a resolve in the set of his jaw. He looked at us earnestly, passion burning in his deep set eyes.

"For some eight years I have been the captain of the Andrea Morgan, a freighter out of Portsmouth. Until recently, we have been transporting mostly raw materials — iron ore, pig iron, lumber, building supplies, that kind of thing. Our route takes us to the continent and various locations around the British Isles."

"You said until recently?" Holmes interrupted. "Something has changed?"

"About six months ago I took on a journey to the Far East — the spice trade is booming just now, and I was offered twice my usual fee to transport tea and spices back to London, which I did gladly."

"Interesting," Holmes remarked.

"You think it is significant?"

"Any change in routine is potentially of interest. And you have made these trips how often since then?"

"Twice. Always at twice my usual fee, and always with the same cargo — tea and spices. I was always paid half in advance and half upon delivery."

"With whom did you make the arrangement, if you don't mind my asking?"

"My first mate, Snead, acted as go-between."

"I see. And how long has this man been in your employment?"

"About seven months. I had a man who had been with me for years, but he vanished suddenly. It was very odd — I would have trusted him with my life, but then one day he didn't report to duty, and I haven't seen hide nor hair of him since."

"That is very odd indeed," Holmes replied. "And your ship — how large a crew do you have?"

The captain paused for me to refill his glass, which he drained once again in one swallow.

"We carry a crew of five: myself, my first mate, and three others, which of late has included my son, Andrew."

Holmes raised an eyebrow. "Your son works for you?"

"Yes, but the arrangement is purely temporary. He is a bright boy, and wants to go to university to study science. I support him in this — as did my dear Elizabeth . . ." His face took on a dreamy expression, and he stared off into the distance for a few moments. Then he seemed to come out of it, and turned back to us.

"I'm sorry — what was I saying?"

"You were telling us about your son," I answered.

"Oh, yes — Andrew. He came to work for me when . . . well, after Elizabeth died. I'm afraid I rather fell apart for a while, and I found it difficult to rise to the challenges of daily life. I . . . I'm embarrassed to admit it, but I stopped caring about anything, and found even the simplest tasks daunting. Andrew stepped in and made sure that the business was conducted — in fact, he probably saved us from the poorhouse."

"I see," said Holmes. "How did your wife die, if you don't mind my asking?"

Captain Crane looked into the flickering flames of the fire as the shadows danced on the wall behind him.

"She contracted food poisoning."

"And you say this happened how long ago?"

"Three months. Some bad stew . . . in fact, if it hadn't been for Jock, I would have probably died with her."

"Jock?" I said. "The dog that you mentioned before?"

"Yes. He got out just as we were sitting down to dinner. I ran after him, you see, and told Elizabeth to go ahead and begin eating without me. When I returned I found her . . ." He put his head in his hands, unable to continue.

"Where was your son at the time?" Holmes asked.

"He was over at a friend's house. We . . . we'd had a fight that night. Thank god for that," he added. "I don't know if I could bear losing both of them . . ."

"What did you fight over?"

The captain shrugged. "The usual things that fathers and strong-willed sons fight over . . . I don't even remember now."

"And now you believe you are seeing your wife's ghost?" Holmes said.

"Yes." Crane leaned forward, elbows on his knees. "I know it sounds unbelievable . . . I can scarcely believe it myself. The first time it happened, I put it down to my frayed nerves and guilt over her death. The second time, I wondered seriously if I was losing my mind. Now I just want to find out what is going on — I'm at a loss to explain it."

"Has anyone else seen this apparition?"

Crane shook his head. "No, not to my knowledge."

"And where does this — visitation — take place?"

"On board my ship, in the middle of the night. I awaken from a deep sleep to find her hovering at the foot of my bed."

"I see. Does she speak?"

"No. She just — looks as me, with those great dark eyes of hers."

"And you are certain it is your wife?"

"Her image is blurry — and I'm always awakening from a deep sleep . . . but it's her hair, her eyes; I even recognize the dress she's wearing."

"Is it possible someone took your wife's dress and is using it?"

"I gave away all her dresses shortly after she . . . I couldn't bear having them around." He looked at Holmes earnestly. "I am not a fanciful man, Mr Holmes."

"Yes, so I observe."

"So you can imagine how this has upset me."

"And this only happens on board your ship?"

"Yes. I have a house in Portsmouth, but I have not experienced anything out of the ordinary there."

"What you tell me is most intriguing, Captain. I will be glad to take on your case."

The captain exhaled, as though he had been holding his breath for a very long time, and his whole body seemed to relax.

"Thank you, Mr Holmes. Thank you," he said, rubbing his eyes wearily.

"You look as though you haven't slept much of late," I remarked.

He nodded. "You are observant as well, Dr Watson. After some nights I awaken with the most dreadful headaches."

"Those would not happen to be the same nights upon which you are visited by your nocturnal spirit, would they?" Holmes inquired.

"Yes, I suppose they are," the captain answered. "I never really thought about it. What does it mean, do you think?"

"That I cannot answer for certain," Holmes replied. "But it is safe to say that it is suggestive, to say the least."

"Well, I will be grateful for any help you can give me in unraveling this strange matter. As to the matter of payment —"

Holmes raised a hand to stop him. "It is of no consequence. I have recently finished a case for a very wealthy client . . . I'm sure we'll be able to come to a satisfactory arrangement. Where are you staying in London?"

"At the Clarion Arms."

"Yes, I know it. I will be in touch soon."

Captain Crane rose from his chair and extended his hand to each of us. "I can hardly express my gratitude to you both." Once again, I was struck by the strength of his grip.

"Save your gratitude for the completion of my investigation," Holmes replied dryly. "Unless I am mistaken, this will prove to be a most challenging case."

"Then I am confident there is no better man in London to get to the bottom of it," Crane replied, moving gracefully to the door. For such a tall man, his economy of movement was striking — a result, perhaps, of his years on shipboard. "Good night to you both."

"Good night," I said, closing the door behind him.

"Well, Watson, what an intriguing mystery, don't you think?" Holmes said after the captain had gone.

"We're not going to the Lake District, are we?" I said.

"Oh, we may make it up there by the week's end, if all goes well," he replied.

"Still, I'd better cable my wife not to expect us."

"Yes, I suppose so."

I sighed. I could tell his mind was already at work on the problem before him — he had quite forgotten about our walking vacation. Never had I seen anyone so indifferent to what most regard as the pleasures of life — a being so perfectly dedicated to his work. He leaned back in his chair and crossed his long legs.

"Consider the facts, Watson. We have a man not given to fanciful thinking who nonetheless believes he experienced a ghostly visitation from the other world, as it were."

"Quite."

"Yet we agree that such things are implausible, at best. Do you not find it instructive, Watson, that shortly after the captain changes his accustomed route, his wife dies under suspicious circumstances?"

"Are you suspicious of her death, Holmes?"

"With poison one must always take a good look around at all possible explanations — not to mention motives."

"So you think she was poisoned?"

"I think the close timing of these various events is suggestive, to say the least. Consider, Watson: Captain Crane acquires a new first mate after the unexplained disappearance of a man who had served him faithfully for years. He then alters his accustomed shipping route after many years of the same routine. Shortly afterwards, his wife falls victim to what is ascribed to food poisoning — ascribed, mind you, but there is no criminal investigation. Then, the captain is visited by her 'spirit' . . . does it not seem like an unusual series of events to be more than mere coincidence?"

"Well, now that you put it like that, Holmes, it does seem suspicious."

"Often when investigating crime, if one looks at the interruption of a routine, one can find the origin of the crime. The moment of interruption often contains the first important clue to the unraveling of the crime."

"I see. So where does that leave us?"

Holmes stood and poured himself a cup of tea.

"Research, Watson — research."

"What kind of research?"

Holmes picked up the magazine I had been reading when our visitor arrived. It was still open to the article on spiritualism. He studied it for a moment before tossing it on the table.

"I suggest we go on a little outing."

"Where to?"

"To a séance, of course! Perhaps some of our questions will be answered there."

I stared at him.

"A *séance*?"

He smiled. "Perhaps your wife's interest will come in handy after all. Come along, then — we may have time for a quick bite at Simpson's if we don't tarry."

An hour or so later I found myself seated beside Holmes in a hansom cab as it rattled along the cobblestone, jolting the roast lamb and potatoes in my stomach that I had hurriedly consumed at Simpson's. The rain that had been looming over the city like a dark promise had finally let loose, and thick bands of showers pelted the streets, making such a din on the roof of our cab that Holmes and I practically had to shout at each other to make ourselves heard.

"So what do you expect to find at the séance?" I said as the cab hit an enormous puddle, sending a spray of water in all directions. A small group of men huddled miserably under the eaves of a bank building, stranded by the sudden downpour, their overcoats slick and glistening, black and wet as seals. I pitied anyone out on the streets tonight — it was no time to be caught without an umbrella.

"I don't know what I'll find, or even that it will be useful, but we shall see soon enough," Holmes replied. "It seems we have arrived at our destination."

Sure enough, the cab was pulling up in front of a handsome townhouse, the home of one Mrs Seidelmore, a widowed lady of some years, and — or so the article had claimed — one of the most popular mediums in London.

The townhouse was in a fashionable part of town; all of the other houses on the block had the smug, comfortable feel of prosperity, snug and solid and successful as their owners. The article had mentioned that Mrs Seidelmore was usually booked well in advance, but we had decided to take a chance that she would include us in tonight's séance.

"We just may be in luck," Holmes said as we climbed the stairs up to the front door. "On a night like this there are bound to be some people who fail to show up."

We were met at the door by a woman of indeterminate age whose face so resembled a piece of dried fruit that her eyes, nose and mouth looked as though they were an afterthought, grafted onto her creviced face at the last minute. She informed us that Mrs Seidelmore was indeed seldom available on such short notice, but as the inclement weather had forced several people to stay in tonight, the august lady would grant us a place at her séance table. We gave our names as Messrs Watkins and Soames, in case Holmes' growing fame might compromise our anonymity.

We were led through a beaded curtain into a cozy parlour at the back of the house. Heavy brocade burgundy curtains hung over the windows, keeping out what little light from the street lamps struggled to get through, and the gas lights were turned down low. A silver candelabra graced the sideboard, throwing shadows on the wall behind us.

Seated around a large round oak table were four people, whom the prune-faced assistant duly introduced to us. There was a retired army officer, Colonel Bloodworth, complete with mutton chop whiskers and an upper class stutter, an elderly pair of Episcopalian nuns from Basingstoke, and a thin, sad-looking young woman dressed all in black. When she was introduced to us as Miss Gallin, she nodded politely but didn't speak.

The elderly sisters excused themselves for a moment and left the room, and the colonel took the opportunity to address us in a friendly, loquacious manner. The red flush in his cheeks and the eager shine in his eyes led me to the conclusion that his conversation was aided by a rather abundant fortification of fermented lubricant.

"I s-s-say, my good fellows, what brings you out on a night like this? B-b-bloody wretched w-w-weather, what? B-b-begging your pardon, Miss," he added quickly, addressing the pale young woman, who shook her head wanly and sighed.

"It is rather beastly out, isn't it?" Holmes responded cheerfully. He was not the most sociable of men, but I could see that he was enjoying himself. Perhaps the use of an alias gave him a certain freedom — rather like an actor donning a character who has a fuller range of expression than he himself might normally display.

The sisters soon returned, and the assistant dimmed the gas lights until the only light in the room came from the single silver candelabra on the sideboard. I detected a faint aroma of sandalwood in the air.

Mrs Seidelmore made her entrance, slipping through the brocade curtains to stand before us. She was a tiny woman with egg shell white skin and the palest eyes I have ever seen. I suppose I was expecting someone dark and exotic — perhaps a gypsy of some kind, heavily made up, laden with cheap jewelry and musky perfume — but my expectations were completely at odds with the lady herself. She was dressed in a simple black robe with the insignia of a red dragon on the back. Her pale hair — blonde or white, I couldn't tell — was pulled back into a severe bun at the nape of her neck, and she wore neither jewelry nor makeup, although she did smell faintly of rose water. Likewise, her age was impossible to guess — perhaps forty, perhaps sixty. In the candlelight her skin appeared unwrinkled and smooth, but her manner suggested someone older.

"Now then," she said, "shall we begin?" Her voice was light and pleasant and decidedly upper crust. I found myself wondering what an educated lady of means was doing in such a setting, but my mind was soon brought back to the matter at hand.

"I want you all to join hands," she intoned solemnly.

We had been seated at the table alternating man/woman/man, so that the men were between two women and vice versa. I was between the pale young woman and one of the elderly sisters. The sister's hand was cool and dry as rice flour, but Miss Gallin's palm was moist and warm. The room was quite cool, so I could only imagine it was emotion that caused her to perspire — anticipation, perhaps even a little fear.

"At no point must this link of hands be broken — *at no point*! If it is, the consequences could be dire," Mrs Seidelmore warned. I felt my own stomach tighten as she lowered her head and continued to speak, this time in a low and thrilling voice.

"Oh, spirits of you who have passed onto the other side, hear me now as I call to you!"

She paused for breath and I could hear the hiss of raindrops outside the house.

"Come now, departed ones, and show us your presence!"

I felt a gust of wind at my back, and one of the candles on the candelabra went out. I tried to make out the expression on Holmes' face, but he was seated across from me, his face in shadow. Miss Gallin's hand closed tightly around mine. I thought I heard a faint distant tinkling of wind chimes.

"There is one struggling to come through," Mrs Seidelmore said. "He is seeking one called Alice — Alex — no, Alicia!"

At that moment Miss Gallin gave a squeak like a mouse and began to rise from her chair.

Do not break the circle!" Mrs Seidelmore commanded sharply, and Miss Gallin sank back down into her chair.

"His name is George . . . and he is on the other side," the medium continued. "Will you show yourself, George?"

Again Miss Gallin tightened her grip on my hand, and began whimpering softly to herself.

"Will you manifest a physical body, George?" the medium repeated.

Everyone in the room waited for the answer with held breath, and I felt a tingle of anticipation creep up my spine. There was another gust of wind, a swooshing sound, and the wavery, luminous figure of a man appeared at the far end of the room. He gave off an eerie greenish glow, and it was hard to see him in detail, though I could make out that he wore a suit and cravat, with a bowler hat pulled low over his eyes.

I have to say that I was impressed by the effect, however it was achieved. Miss Gallin, however, was stunned by it.

"George!" she cried.

At that the ghostly form reached his arms out toward her, whereupon she gave a pathetic whimper and promptly fainted. The apparition stared at her for a moment, then vanished, until all that was left was a wispy greenish glow. The rest of us sat there, momentarily taken aback by what we had seen, and then I shook myself out of my daze and felt Miss Gallin's pulse. To my relief, it was quite strong and steady — as I suspected, the young lady had merely fainted.

Then Mrs Seidelmore spoke.

"I believe we have had enough for one evening," she said in a firm voice, and rose from the table to turn up the gas lamps. "Will

Miss Gallin be all right?" she asked me, seeing that I was minis-
tering to her.

"Yes," I replied. "She has just fainted. Perhaps a bit of whis-
key would help her recover."

The elderly sisters exchanged a glance at my mention of the
more mundane form of spirits, but the colonel seemed cheered by
it.

"I say, b-bloody good idea, old chap!"

"I think perhaps we could all do with some refreshment," Mrs
Seidelmore suggested as her parched faced assistant appeared at
the door.

Miss Gallin stirred and moaned a bit, then gave a little
shudder and opened her eyes.

"It's all right," I said, doing my best to soothe her rattled
nerves.

"Come along, dear," the assistant said, taking her firmly by
the shoulders and escorting her into the front parlour. "We'll get
you a nice cup of tea and some biscuits, and soon you'll feel much
better."

"Will she be all right?" Holmes whispered to me as we lingered behind the others.

"Yes. She just had a nasty shock."

The colonel approached me and nudged me in the elbow. "I
say, that was quite something, eh w-what?"

"Yes, quite," I replied with a glance at Holmes. He was
standing near the tall armoire, the spot where "Georgie" had ma-
terialized.

"I'm so disappointed — my friend so wanted to contact dear
departed Mrs Watkins," he remarked to Mrs Seidelmore, who
was standing in the doorway between the two rooms. "Didn't you,
Watkins?"

"W-why, yes — yes, I did," I said.

"Poor dear," Mrs Seidelmore responded.

"Yes, I — I miss her very much," I replied.

"Yes, they were very close when she was alive," Holmes went
on. "Why don't you tell Mrs Seidelmore about her?" Clearly he
wanted me to distract the good lady so that he could have a quick
look around the room.

The medium looked at me, sympathy pulling at the corners of
her pale blue eyes. "How long ago did she pass on?"

"Oh . . . five years," I answered, hoping I was a convincing liar.
"But it feels like yesterday," I added quickly, taking her arm in
mine and following after the others into the back parlour. She
glanced behind her at Holmes, but I pulled her firmly forward.

"Yes," I said sadly, "she meant the world to me, my . . . Edith."

I have no idea where the name came from, as my wife's name is Mary.

"I see you still wear your wedding ring," Mrs Seidelmore observed, glancing at my left hand, which I had wrapped securely around her elbow.

"Oh — yes," I responded. "My friends tell me I should move on, think of marrying again, but for me there is only Edith."

She nodded and patted my arm. "Yes, yes, that's how it is for some of us." Her voice was so kind and sincere that I felt a pang of guilt that Holmes and I were deceiving her. Even though I suspected her to be a deceiver herself, it was one thing to know it and quite another to be in her presence, warm and inviting as a spring day.

We joined the others in the back parlour, where the elderly sisters were mothering Miss Gallin, clucking soothingly and plying her with tea and biscuits. The major had found the liquor cabinet, and was happily pouring himself a Scotch and soda.

To my immense relief, Holmes joined us moments later.

"Your friend was telling us about his loss," Mrs Seidelmore said as he entered the room.

"Yes, yes, poor Mrs Watkins, left us just a year ago," he said sadly.

She looked at me. "But I thought you said —"

"My *mother* died a year ago," I answered quickly. "My *wife* has been gone for five years now."

I glared at Holmes. The corners of his mouth twitched, but he nodded solemnly.

"Yes, quite."

"You poor thing," one of the elderly sisters said.

Mrs Seidelmore poured us a cup of tea and turned to Miss Gallin. "Are you all right, dear?"

Miss Gallin nodded, sniffling.

"I must say, I did not expect quite such an emotional reaction," the medium remarked.

"Is it unusual, then?" Holmes inquired.

"Unusual, perhaps, though not unheard of. Most people are more — prepared, shall we say? — for the appearance of their loved departed ones."

"That was him — Georgie, my dear brother Georgie!" Miss Gallin sobbed as they dabbed away her tears with lavender scented lace handkerchiefs.

After a quick cup of tea, we made our excuses, with a promise to return soon to try again. I noticed that even though the session had been somewhat truncated, the good medium's fee was not waived or reduced. Business, it seemed, was business.

Later, in the cab on the way home, Holmes leaned back in the upholstered seat and closed his eyes. "Ah, the power of suggestion, Watson — people see what they expect to see, and believe what they want to believe. Unlikely as it seems, there is most certainly a link between our sea captain and that poor girl."

"Yes," I replied. "Because of the state he is in — depressed, exhausted, in the throes of grief — his mind is highly vulnerable and receptive to suggestion. Like Miss Gallin, he wishes to believe that his wife's ghost could be walking the ship. It isn't the same as having her there in the flesh, but to his grief-stricken mind it's the next best thing."

"Well said, Watson — you have explained it admirably, I think. After all, which of us would not like to think that our beloved departed are still with us, waiting on some other plane of existence? It does make this life seem less lonely, less final, does it not?"

"I suppose it does at that. But still, people deliberately allowing themselves to be duped, suspending all critical sense, all skepticism . . ."

Holmes smiled. "You are a man of science, Watson, rigorously trained in the laws of Nature, of cause and effect. And I am by nature a skeptic — and I have trained myself in the art of observation. But we do not represent the majority of the populace. The average person is more driven by what he *wants* than by what *is*. Desire to believe plays a more important part in people's views than logic and reason."

"Of course, you're right," I replied. "But what of these charlatans who play to the hopes of people like Miss Gallin?"

Holmes shrugged. "Well, they are hardly honest. But are they doing so much damage, after all? It was a comfort to Miss Gallin to think her dead brother's spirit has spoken to her from beyond the grave, was it not?"

"But they are defrauding people, taking their money —"

"True. But I am constantly amazed at what foolish ways people have of spending their money."

"So do you know how she accomplished it?"

"I have a reasonable idea. Of course, our shipboard ghost may be somewhat more improvised than this one was . . . not having control of every variable makes a difference."

"One can never have control of every variable, surely."

"Precisely, Watson. As to this shipboard haunting, we shall see . . ." He turned to me and smiled. "And perhaps we shall find it is a spirit, after all."

"Holmes, you just finished lecturing me on the nature of belief and trickery. I don't believe you could convince me that you really believe in the possibility of spirits."

"Perhaps not. But still, there are more things in heaven and hell, Watson, than are dreamed of —"

"Don't you mean heaven and earth?"

He smiled grimly. "I believe that, in this case, hell is a more appropriate word. There are darker forces at work here, Watson, forces even I am not entirely aware of."

I looked out at the raindrops hurtling themselves against our window panes. The sky glowered as bulky grey clouds settled over the sooty London skyline.

When I arose the next morning, Holmes was already out, and he returned to find me seated at the breakfast table, pouring myself a cup of coffee. He looked ruddy-cheeked and invigourated, and carried a brown paper-wrapped package underneath his arm.

"Nothing like a brisk walk before breakfast to stimulate the appetite, eh, Watson?" he said, seating himself across from me at the table.

"Where have you been?" I asked, intrigued by the package at his feet.

"Ah, yes — that. Here, Watson," he said, tossing the bundle at me, "do your best to transform yourself from a respectable doctor into a deck hand."

I opened the bundle. It was an assortment of clothes, most of them well-worn, by the looks of it. There was a pair of rough cut breeches, an open-throated white cotton shirt, and a short blue wool jacket.

"I believe I got your size about right," Holmes remarked as he poured himself a cup of coffee.

"What's this about, Holmes?"

"I have been studying shipboard life, Watson, and I have learned quite a few things that I found interesting and even surprising."

"Such as — ?"

But my question was interrupted by the arrival of Mrs Hudson, who appeared at the door, carrying a steaming platter. The aroma of Canadian bacon wafted across the room.

"Your breakfast, gentlemen," she announced rather triumphantly.

"Capital, Mrs Hudson!" Holmes barked. I had noticed that lack of sleep, rather than making him lethargic, often had the opposite effect — for a while, at any rate, until it caught up with him.

"We're going incognito, Watson," Holmes said after Mrs Hudson had left. "Into the belly of the beast, as it were."

The meaning of his words dawned on me. "You mean we're going to pose as sailors on the Andrea Morgan?"

"What else? The presence of an investigating detective and his colleague would drive our quarry further underground — hardly the way to solve our case, don't you agree?"

"I suppose," I answered dubiously, looking at the pile of clothing. The physician in me didn't care even to speculate as to where they came from.

"Oh, come now, Watson," Holmes said, seeing my glum face. "Where's your sense of adventure?"

I shrugged. Right now I wished I were sitting inside a snug hotel in the Lake District, a bottle of single malt at my side.

"How are your shipboard skills?" Holmes inquired, plucking a muffin from the basket on the table.

"Well, I did spend some time on board a ship during my stint in the army, as you know. But that was a long time ago . . ."

"Well, Watson, are you game?"

I sighed. "I'll do my best."

Mrs Hudson returned moments later with fresh coffee. All throughout breakfast she did not attempt to conceal her surprise at seeing Holmes up and about at such an unusual hour; she muttered a bit to herself about "irregular habits" as she served us our oatmeal and eggs, and shook her head as she cleared the table. The good landlady had a touch of the dramatic about her, which perhaps was why she was able to tolerate my friend's eccentricities. As we left she pressed a package of sandwiches into my hands.

"It's a raw day out there, and God knows when he'll remember to eat next, Dr Watson. Take these just in case."

I thanked her and set out after Holmes, who was already down in the street hailing a cab. I hurried down the stairs after him and stepped out into the street. Steam swirled up from the damp streets; the storm had passed through in the night, making way for a cool, bright day, and now that the temperature of the ground was warmer than the air, a foggy mist rose from the cobblestones.

On the way to the docks Holmes filled me in as best he could as to the ways of shipboard life. Fortunately, I had some experience aboard transport chips as a soldier — still, I had no great confidence that I would be able to pull off our deception.

When we arrived at the docks it was just after nine o'clock. The tremendous deluge of the day before had done little to suppress the usual hustle and bustle in England's most populous port. The piers were crawling with dock workers, sailors, deck hands, day labourers, scavengers, financiers and their servants. The scene reminded me of the activity in a bee hive or an ant hill — the constant comings and going, the incessant buzz and hum of activity seemed as instinctive and unconscious as a swarm of insects.

We soon found the Andrea Morgan. She was a mid-sized freighter, painted a rust-coloured red with blue trim. She looked to be in pretty good shape for a ship that had evidently seen some years of service.

Captain Crane was supervising the loading of cargo when we arrived, and as soon as he saw us he came over to greet us.

"Thank you for coming, Mr Holmes — Dr Watson," he said, shaking both our hands vigorously.

In the morning light his face was no less handsome; in fact, he looked less care-worn than he had the previous night. Perhaps the knowledge that the great Sherlock Holmes was at his service had eased his mind. In the bright, hazy sunlight his eyes were a cloudy sea green.

"I hope we can be of some service, Captain," Holmes replied, looking at a couple of sailors in starched white uniforms, fresh off their ship on leave, their caps set jauntily to one side on their heads. They strode by full of youth and adventure and expectation, leaning eagerly into their future as though nothing evil could befall them.

"Oh, I'd like you to meet my son." Captain Crane said. "Andrew! Come over here a minute, will you?" he called to a tall, black haired youth of about eighteen, who was overseeing the loading of a stack of crates. The boy walked over to us, hands in his pockets, a sulky expression on his face. He clearly took after his father, with the same curly black hair and deep-set eyes, yet his face was more delicate, almost girlish, with full, chubby lips. One could sense his mother's influence in the more compact build and delicate bone structure of his face.

"These are our two new deck hands, Watkins and Soames," Captain Crane said, putting a hand on his son's shoulder.

"How d'you do?" the boy said, without offering either of us his hand. He was clearly not pleased to see us, and I couldn't help wondering why.

His father frowned, but before he could reprimand the boy, a red-haired man came over to greet us. He was short and powerfully built; his bare arms bulged with tattoos of mermaids, anchors and sea creatures. A large green sea serpent dominated his left bicep; its long, scaly tail wrapped around his sinuous wrist.

"Hello there!" he said cheerfully, pushing back the knitted wool cap he wore over his closely cropped hair, which was the colour of ripened winter wheat. His beard, also neatly clipped, was a brighter shade of red, almost orange. With his ruddy, sunburnt skin and pale blue eyes, he cut a striking figure, even among the collection of colourful characters swarming all around us.

"This is my first mate, Samuel Snead," Captain Crane said. "You'll be working under him. Snead, these are the men I told you about — Watkins and Soames."

Snead reached out to shake our hands, and I noticed that part of his thumb and index finger was missing on his right hand. From the scar tissue that had formed over the stumps, I surmised that his deformity was the result of an accident rather than a birth defect. He appeared entirely unselfconscious about it, however, and began chattering cheerfully with us.

"Done much work on freighters, have you?" he asked, sizing us up with a practiced eye.

"Not much," Holmes replied. "But Captain Crane was kind enough to give us a try, and here we are."

"You'll not find a more capable skipper this side of the Channel," Snead said. "Come along, lads, and I'll show you around." Then, noticing that I was looking at his mangled hand, he winked at me. "Barracuda, off the coast of Saint Thomas. Ever been to the West Indies?"

"No, I can't say that I have," I replied.

"Most beautiful beaches I ever seen. The sea there is turquoise, warm and clear as crystal. But watch out for the barracuda. They'll just as soon take a chunk out of you as look at you. Ugly buggers, too," he added with a grin. "Teeth like razors. Well, come on, let's go — we're burnin' daylight standing around runnin' our mouths!"

Later, after we had received a tour of the ship, Holmes and I stood together on the deck watching Snead supervise the dock workers as they loaded freight onto the ship.

"I'll wager he's done time, Watson," Holmes murmured.

"Really?"

"I have seen that sea serpent design before on the arms of inmates of Braxton Prison."

"Indeed. I wonder if Captain Crane knows about his first mate's past?"

Holmes shook his head. "I doubt that someone like the captain would be entirely innocent of the matter. After all, probably half of the men who serve on shipboard are former convicts."

By half past eleven the cargo had been loaded and we set off for Portsmouth. I was assigned to the engine room, which suited me just fine. The head mechanic, Gubbins, was an affable giant who spoke little but laughed easily. With his shiny bullet-shaped head and enormous torso set on rather spindly legs, he resembled a bulldog; luckily for me, he also had the open, friendly nature of that breed. My duties were not demanding; mostly I was required to see that the ship's furnace remained stoked with coal, but that the temperature did not exceed a safe level.

Holmes, on the other hand, was to act as ship's navigator. As long as we were still cruising along the Thames, this presented little challenge, I supposed, though I had no idea what he planned to do once we hit open water. He had gained a working knowledge of the constellations during his work on "The Case of the Star-Struck Astronomer," but it was one thing to know the positions of the stars and quite another to navigate by them. I had no doubt Captain Crane knew much of the route by heart; the important thing was that Holmes convince the rest of the crew of his abilities.

Besides the ship's cook, the only other crewman aboard was Crane's son, Andrew. As far as I could tell, he was in charge of the paper-work; he also looked after the cargo and filled in at any of the dozen odd jobs that come up aboard a freighter. The boy's surly manner did not disappear entirely, but he now nodded to me civilly when we passed in the corridor. Except for the captain and the cook, we all took turns swabbing the deck and performing other routine cleaning tasks, which I thought very democratic of our skipper.

The first day passed without incident, and by that night I was so exhausted from the unaccustomed manual labour that my head barely touched the pillow before I sank into a deep sleep. The night shift in the engine room was to be shared between Gubbins and Andrew, and the steering of the vessel was broken into three shifts: the captain, Snead and Holmes would each take their turn at the wheel while the others slept.

Holmes had specifically requested a night shift — to keep an eye on things, I supposed — and the schedule no doubt suited his nocturnal nature; many a time I had known him to sit up smoking his Haverstraw pipe all night, only to retire to bed at the first rays of morning light.

Lulled by the gentle rolling motion of the ship, I slept like the dead on the first night, awakening to the smell of coffee drifting up from the galley. The fresh sea air and exercise had given me a terrific appetite, and I ate enough for two men. After a hearty breakfast of sausage and slap jacks, I headed off to my post in the engine room.

As I headed for the steep steps that led down to the engine room, Holmes caught up with me and pulled me aside.

"Within a day's journey we will be in open sea," he said in a low voice, glancing down the corridor to make sure we were alone. "Therefore, I believe that tonight he will make his move. After that, weather conditions and rough water will make it more difficult."

"Really?" I whispered. "What do you intend to do?"

"This is my plan: you will take the place of Captain Crane in his bed tonight, and he will take your bed. No one will know of this except for us, and we will make the switch at midnight, the beginning of the second watch."

"What am I to do?"

"Just pretend to be asleep. Don't worry — I will be nearby, in case anything does happen."

"Very well," I said.

"There is something else of interest I'd like you to see."

"Really? What's that?"

"This way," he replied, and led me down the stairs past the engine room to the aft hull where the cargo was stored. It was a low-ceilinged, dingy room, and smelled of moss and mildew. It was stacked wall to wall with crates and crates of tea.

"Here," he said, lighting a torch he had brought for the purpose. "What do you see?" he said, holding the torch low over the rows of crates stacked upon the floor.

I bent down to examine them. The first thing that struck me was that, along with the smell of tea and mildew, was another smell — a sweet, sickly odour.

I stood up. "There is something in these crates other than tea, isn't there?"

He nodded. "Just so, Watson — as I suspected, we have come upon the reason for all the deception and skullduggery. Unless I am mistaken, there is opium in these crates."

"Smuggling!"

"Precisely."

"But who? Clearly the captain is unaware, or he would — ?"

Holmes shook his head. "I don't know. And for the present, I can't entirely leave the captain out of the equation. These are deep waters, Watson, and I suspect there is another player whose hand is visible — but who lurks in the shadows, as usual."

I stared at him in dim light. "Not — ?"

He nodded. "I can't be certain, but I suspect that my old enemy Moriarty is behind this. I know that he has been steadily infiltrating the shipping business in and out of London; I believe it is his master plan to maintain a stranglehold on the docks, so that he can smuggle drugs in and out at his leisure. This has the mark of his hand."

My skin went cold, and I felt my heart beating in my throat at the mention of Moriarty's name. "That would mean one of his agents is aboard this ship."

Holmes nodded. "Just so, Watson. Which is why we cannot consider anyone above suspicion, and that is why we must maintain a constant vigilance."

Just then I heard footsteps approaching the cargo storage area. Holmes hurried along the corridor in the opposite direction as I tried to duck into the stairwell just as the first mate came around the corner. He saw me, though, and stopped to talk with me.

"Hello there, Watkins," he said, looking me up and down.

His red hair glinted in the sun, the early morning rays bringing out the copper highlights. His eyes were of the palest blue, so that they were almost translucent. I was suddenly reminded of a pair of favourite marbles I'd had as a child, light blue and glassy as the irises of his eyes. He stood in front of me, his muscular arms flexed, so that the tattoos on his biceps bulged. The tale of the sea serpent on his left arm waved at me, and the beast's grin widened into a lascivious smirk.

"How are you farin' on board the Andrea Morgan, then?" Snead asked. His voice was friendly enough, but there was an edge behind it, a suggestion of a threat, the hint of barely repressed violence.

"Oh, very well, thank you," I replied. I felt the sweat prickle on the back of my neck. The man's voice and manner unsettled me, and I hoped I was hiding it successfully.

"That's good," he said. "You know it's funny, but you and yer friend don't talk much like sailors."

"No, I suppose not, "I answered, attempting a laugh, which came out rather poorly, as if I were suffering from indigestion or something. "But then, neither does Captain Crane," I added quickly, as the thought struck me.

"Yes, he's quite the educated fellow, ain't he?" the mate replied, cocking his head to one side and sucking on a bit of toothpick sticking out of the left side of his mouth. He plucked the tooth-pick from his lips with his mangled hand, grasping it deftly between the remaining fingers. I was struck by how quickly Nature adapts to catastrophe and loss; I had noticed him at work around the ship, and the dexterity of his crippled hand was no less than that of many able-bodied men I have seen. His total lack of self-consciousness about the disfigurement was impressive, too — he seemed almost to enjoy the effect it had on people. I tried to make of a point of not staring at the hand, but he saw me glance at it and winked at me. There was something unpleasant and vulgar about that wink, a suggestion of familiarity that I would not have sought with someone such as him.

"At least there are no barracudas in the Thames, eh, Watkins?" he said, grinning broadly, displaying strong white teeth, no doubt bleached from years of sun and salt water. "But," he added, "you never know what you'll find lurkin' under the waves, so it's best to be watchful, eh?"

"Yes, I suppose so," I murmured. "Now, if you'll excuse me, I must get on with my duties."

There passed a frightening moment when I thought he would not move out of the way, but then his face relaxed and he stepped aside.

"Right you are," he said cheerfully, letting me pass. I hurried down the stairs to the engine room, glad to be rid of his company.

Later that day, as I was heading up to the galley for a cup of a tea, I overheard raised voices coming from the captain's cabin. I recognized the first voice as belonging to Captain Crane, and I couldn't be sure, but I thought the other one belonged to his son, Andrew. I lingered outside of the door for a few moments, and I was able to overhear some of the conversation.

"What has gotten into you?" the captain said. I could hear him pacing about the cabin, obviously agitated.

"Just *say* it! Just *tell* me!"

"There's nothing to tell!"

"I don't believe you!"

Just then I heard someone else coming, and I ducked around the corner before I could be spotted. I resolved to tell Holmes what I had overheard as soon as I could.

That night we ate in shifts; the captain dined alone with Holmes and myself, as the others attended to their various duties.

"How is your head, Captain?" I inquired.

"Much better, thank you," he replied, draining his glass of wine. Alcohol was not rationed on the Andrea Morgan, I noticed; beer and ale were served with lunch, and the captain drank wine with dinner.

"I believe tonight is to be the night," Holmes said as we tucked into a beef and kidney pie. The ship's cook did a credible beef and kidney pie, though the roast leg of mutton of the previous night was not up to Mrs Hudson's standards.

"Now, this is what I'd like you to do," Holmes continued, explaining the plan he had outlined to me earlier in the day.

"Very well," the captain agreed, "but I hope this isn't putting Dr Watson in any danger."

"I shall be close by at all times," Holmes replied. "And with any luck, we will get to the bottom of this business tonight."

The captain's mood was much lifted by this, and as the meal progressed and we all continued to partake of his excellent bottle of Bordeaux, he grew quite expansive. We spoke of many things — of philosophy and politics, of progress and profanity. As we talked, the ship's cat made an appearance; sauntering into the room, it rubbed itself against the captain's shins. It was an odd little creature, a dark, almost black tabby with a long, pointed nose and unusually large ears, so that its face rather resembled a bat.

"I hope you don't mind my saying this," I remarked, "but you seem unusually well educated for a professional sailor. What made you choose a life at sea, if you don't mind my asking?"

Crane put down his wine glass and studied the crimson liquid inside it.

"Some men are born to life at sea, and some men are called to it, but she is a demanding and jealous mistress. Once caught in her net, few can return to the life they once knew. The sea changes everything; she becomes her own context, the alpha and omega of existence. You rise in the morning with the smell of salt water in your nostrils, and you fall off to bed hearing the sound of the waves in your dreams. That never changes; you can move hundreds of miles inland, but it never changes. Once she's got you, you're hers — and the sea knows that. Her power over men isn't benign, but it demands respect. Respect her, and she just might let you live another day, a week, a month — even another year."

As the captain talked, the cat jumped nimbly onto the table and began picking delicately at the food left on our plates. I looked at Crane, but he didn't appear to notice, so I said nothing.

"You seem to have thought quite a lot about this," Holmes remarked.

The captain shrugged and drained the last of his wine. "Maybe one has to love death a little bit to live this life; I'm not sure. All I know is that once you choose it, it's hard to look at anything else, much as you might want to," he continued, stroking the cat absently. The animal arched its back and walked stiff-legged in a little circle, purring loudly.

It occurred to me at that moment that Captain Crane and Holmes had more in common than I had realized at first; I had often thought my friend had a bit of a death wish, otherwise he would not have chosen so perilous a profession.

Later that night, before the first watch began, I went into the galley on the pretext of needing a glass of water; Holmes and I had agreed to meet there to finalize our plan. I found him waiting for me, standing in the corner by the tins of flour and tea.

"Are you quite ready?" he said, his voice sharp with anticipation.

"Yes, I think so. I am to take the captain's bed, and he is to take mine."

"Yes. You will pretend to be asleep, but remain awake. I hope that does not present too much of a problem for you."

I laughed. "Don't worry — there's no fear of my falling asleep tonight!" Indeed, my nerves were so keyed up that even the Bordeaux I had consumed at dinner seemed to have little effect.

"And where will you be?"

"Close by — but not so close, I hope, that I scare off our prey."

"Very well. I heard something today," I continued, and proceeded to tell him about the argument I had overheard coming from the captain's cabin.

"Hmm," he replied, stroking his chin. "Of some interest, though not unexpected, I think. How odd," he said, suddenly gazing at the tins lined up against the wall.

"What's odd?" I inquired.

"These dead flies."

"What's so odd about dead flies?"

"Not so much the fact that they are dead, but that they are all in the same place. I wonder . . ." he said, beginning to examine the row of tins on the shelf.

But at that moment we heard footsteps, and turned around to see the first mate enter the room.

"All set for your watch, fellows?" he said, with a sharp glance at Holmes, who nodded.

"Certainly."

"You'd best not get into Cookie's things," the mate warned, smiling. "He is a holy terror when anyone messes with his galley."

"I wouldn't dream of it," Holmes replied. "We were just getting a glass of water."

"All right, then, off you go," the mate answered, studying my friend, but Holmes' face was a mask of innocence as we left the room.

I headed toward my quarters, then doubled back on my steps, making sure that no one saw me as I headed for the captain's cabin. The door was ajar, and I slipped into the room unnoticed. As I changed into my nightshirt, I noticed a cup of tea by the bedside. It was quite hot, so I presumed the cook had brought it up to the captain; perhaps it was his custom to drink tea before retiring. As it was a raw night, I drank it down gratefully. It had an odd, musky aroma, but it was hot and sweet and I finished it greedily. I supposed it to be some unfamiliar kind of Chinese tea that the captain had become fond of during his voyages; I preferred a good straight orange pekoe myself, but it was welcome nonetheless on such a cold night.

I climbed into bed, put out the light, and settled down to wait for the appearance of my nocturnal visitor.

In spite of my earlier wakefulness, I was gradually overcome by the pull of a drowsiness unlike any other I had ever known. I was dragged down into disturbing and lurid dreams, in which I was swimming through dark and hazy depths, pursued by horrible sea creatures, their faces alit with malice, their eyes shining red as demons. I heard the ship's clock striking one as I was brought into sudden consciousness — or rather, a form of consciousness. When I opened my eyes I could see the room in the moonlight, which shone a ghostly pale blue through the window — but it was not the room I remembered seeing when I went to bed.

The walls appeared to shift and move before my eyes, as though they were made of some liquid substance, and the shapes of the objects in the room were some twisted version of what I remembered: the clock on the wall seemed to be grinning at me, its white face an evil, malicious mask, the numbers dancing and winking at me. Then, as I watched, the face transformed itself into the form of the sea serpent tattoo on the first mate's arm. The beast twisted and writhed, and opened its cavernous maw, its teeth white and gleaming in the moonlight. It stretched its evil head toward me, its hideous mouth gaping wide as if to devour me. I shrank back in the bed, paralyzed with fear.

My head felt thick and fuzzy, as though it were full of cobwebs, and I could not manage to think clearly. I tried to convince myself that the things I was seeing were impossible, but just then I felt the bedclothes themselves moving of their own volition; I was certain they were going to wrap around my neck and strangle me. I opened my mouth to scream, but just then I heard a whooshing sound and a form appeared at the far end of the room. I squinted to see it more clearly, for it was wavery and luminous. There was no question that it was the figure of a woman, dressed all in white, with long black curls. The apparition lifted an arm toward me, pointing at me with her long, slender hand, and this time I did scream. I was utterly convinced that it was the captain's dead wife, and that she had returned from the grave to avenge her killer.

In my confused state, I believed she thought me responsible for her death, and was there to take her revenge upon me. Though I tried to remain silent, the screams welled up in my throat and forced themselves out of me, as though I had no will of my own. The ghostly figured hesitated, then started towards me, at which point I screamed even louder.

I am not entirely certain what happened next, as my confusion was only deepened by the action around me; the cobwebs inside my head seemed to grow denser and thicker, clouding out any chance of clear thinking. But I was aware of Holmes appearing suddenly in the room, from behind the apparition, and of the sound of voices . . . there was shouting, and the sound of a scuffle, and then a gunshot.

The sound of gunfire brought me more to my senses, though when I tried to move I felt as though I was underwater. I jumped out of bed as quickly as I could, and stumbled to the corner of the room where I had seen the 'ghost,' only to find Holmes lying on the floor against the wall.

"Holmes!" I cried, as Captain Crane entered the room breathlessly. I felt as if everything were happening in slow motion, in another room, and that I was merely observing the events as they occurred before me.

"He got away," Crane said. "Jumped overboard. I saw him swimming towards a skiff . . . he may have made it; he's a strong swimmer. Are you all right?" he said, seeing that Holmes was lying on the floor.

"Yes," Holmes replied, getting to his feet. "It's just a scratch. Where is Andrew?"

"Right here," came the boy's voice from behind the captain.

I looked up, and to my surprise, saw not the boy, but the lady in white, minus her long dark curls. It took my muddled brain a moment to make the connection, but then I realized what had transpired: the apparition of the captain's late wife had in fact been his son — with a wig and makeup, the boy's resemblance to his dead mother was uncanny. His clothes glowed with a peculiar greenish hue, which I recognized as phosphorus. I could see that his eyes had been lined with kohl, and there was rouge upon his cheeks.

The captain evidently had the same question as I did, because he turned to his son.

"Why, Andrew?"

The boy hung his head. "He told me it was your fault she died — that you had poisoned her. He told me that if you saw her ghost you would confess — that you would repent what you had done."

Crane shook his head sadly. "How could you think that of me, Andrew? How could you?"

"I'm sorry," the boy answered softly. "I just — after a while, I just didn't know what to think."

I suddenly realized the significance of the argument I had overheard earlier that day. "Snead?" I asked Holmes, who nodded. My voice sounded odd, as though I were in an echo chamber.

"He poisoned the boy's mind just as surely as he poisoned Mrs Crane."

"Let me look at that, will you?" I said, noticing that Holmes was clutching his shoulder.

"Really, it's nothing, Watson."

I was glad of his response, as my vision was still blurry. I blinked my eyes in an attempt to focus.

"What is it, Watson?" Holmes said. "Are you all right?"

I smiled ruefully. "I'm afraid I may be a bit the worse for wear myself tomorrow." I gestured toward the empty tea cup next to the bed. My head was still swimming, but the hallucinations had ceased, and the shapes around me were returning to normal. "I'm afraid my tea was tampered with."

"Of course!" Holmes cried. "I suspected as much, but I didn't know about the bedtime cup of tea."

"I should have told you," Crane said. "It's been my custom for so many years to drink a cup of herbal tea before retiring that I quite forgot to mention it."

Holmes picked up the cup and sniffed it. "That explains the dead flies in the kitchen."

"Dead flies?" Captain Crane said.

"*Amanita muscaria*," Holmes replied. "It's a mushroom, a member of the deadly amanita family, otherwise known as fly agaric. Very effective at killing flies — and highly hallucinogenic to humans."

"So *that's* how he did it!" Crane exclaimed, seizing the tea cup from Holmes.

"Yes," Holmes agreed. "*Amanita muscaria* produces a confused, hallucinogenic state in the victim. It also can inhibit movement and coherency, so that you were unable to pursue your 'ghostly visitor' while under the influence of the drug." He moved to the closet on the far side of the room and pulled aside the sliding door, which moved noiselessly in its grooves. "Yes," he said, examining it, "this has been recently oiled, so that it will slide back and forth without a sound. A very similar technique was used at the séance we attended in London," he said to me. "I detected the presence of a secret panel in that room that connected with another part of the house, so that the 'apparition' could slip into the room almost soundlessly. Of course," he added, "our London medium did not have the advantage of a drugged audience." He turned to Andrew Crane. "Did you wait in here until your father was asleep?" he said in a severe tone.

The boy nodded, his face a picture of guilt and misery. He still held the wig in his hands. Having never seen her alive, I did not realize how keen the resemblance was between him and his dead mother, but apparently it was strong enough to fool his grieving, drug-afflicted father.

"I don't know what to say. I am so very sorry for my part in this," the boy said forlornly.

"We'll talk about it tomorrow," his father replied sternly, but I could hear the relief in his voice. "Poor Dr Watson," he said, turning to me. "You'd best get to bed — you will undoubtedly have a most unpleasant time of it tomorrow, if your headaches are anything like mine."

The captain's prediction was unfortunately all too true; I awoke the next morning with a thudding headache. At breakfast, I sipped my coffee but could not bear the thought of food.

Captain Crane looked at me sympathetically. "You don't look terribly good, Dr Watson, if you don't mind my saying so."

I rubbed my forehead. "I know now what your headaches have been like."

The captain smiled ruefully. "Yes, I'm sorry about that."

Holmes shook his head. "No, it is I who should apologize. I should have examined your routine more closely; if I had, I would have figured out that on nights when you were to be 'visited' by your late wife's 'ghost,' your tea would be laced with hallucinogens. I was examining the tins in the galley when I was interrupted by the appearance of your first mate. He kept a close eye on me from then on, and it was difficult to shake him."

The captain shook his head. "I just can't understand why

Snead would want to destroy me. I wasn't a bad employer, and we seemed to get on well."

"He was just an agent of someone more malicious and powerful than you can imagine, Captain. It was unfortunate for you that you found yourself between this man and something he wanted."

"What was that?"

"Your ship, and all that went with it — your shipping route, and mostly importantly, the valuable cargo you carried. He is an old and entrenched enemy of mine, and this is not the first time we have locked swords."

"Really? Who is this person?"

"His name is Professor James Moriarty, and I believe him to be behind this entire business."

The captain stared at Holmes. "You amaze me, Mr Holmes."

"I also regret to tell you that, as I suspected earlier, I now believe your wife was poisoned."

"But why? What did she ever do to deserve that?"

"The answer to that is quite simple," Holmes replied. "The poison was not meant for her."

The captain's face went rigid with shock. "Not meant for her? For who, then?"

"It was meant for you."

"Me?"

"Moriarty was intent on gaining control of your ship and its valuable route to the Orient. You were obviously an impediment to that plan. It was simple enough to get your first mate to lace your stew with poison — and, as Moriarty includes a working knowledge of mycology in his bag of many tricks, I suspect he gave Snead an extract of a more deadly amanita than the fly agaric — perhaps the Destroying Angel, or the Death Cap. Either one would mimic symptoms of severe food poisoning, and lead eventually to death. Probably he intended for Snead to poison you and your entire family. But he could not anticipate that you and your son would have an argument that night, and that your son would then leave before dinner — or that your dog would manage to get out and suddenly take off after a rabbit, or a squirrel, or whatever it was he was chasing . . . it is the unanticipated elements that can put a crimp in even the most well thought out plan.

"In any event, that dog saved your life, though your wife was not so lucky. Seeing the effect that her death had upon you, however, Moriarty may have thought that you would succumb to your grief and give up your ship, as it were, allowing him to place one of his henchmen at the helm. But when your son stepped in and took up the reins, Moriarty was forced to try another tack."

"Hence the 'hauntings.'"

"Precisely. You were already close to the breaking point; if he could get you to snap entirely, he could wrest control of your ship. Another poisoning would look too suspicious; likewise, a violent death might draw too much attention. Your grief provided him with an idea; once Snead was able to enlist the help of your son to create the appearance of the 'ghost,' he figured it was a matter of time before you succumbed to the strain of your wife's death and went entirely . . ."

"Mad. He was trying to drive me mad."

"Yes."

Crane shook his head. "You say you have previous experience of this . . . this fiend. How can it be you are still alive?"

Holmes shrugged. "Who can say? Perhaps it is only a matter of time for me as well."

The captain shuddered. "Let us hope not, Mr Holmes. I for one am profoundly grateful that you have returned my ship — and my son — to me. How can I ever thank you?"

Holmes waved his hand dismissively. "Please do not trouble yourself. I have made but a single stab in the effort to make our mutual world more inhabitable . . . though it does me good to see my efforts here were successful, there is still more to be done."

The captain extended his hand. "I will be sending you a check — and, in the meantime, please do take care, as I imagine your enemy, as you call him, will not be pleased that you have defeated his efforts yet again."

Holmes smiled as he took the captain's hand. "No doubt you are right there. But I cannot spend my time worrying about it; there are more important things to attend to."

Later that day, the Andrea Morgan returned to port in London to let us off, and then continued on its journey to Portsmouth.

As we rode home in the cab, Holmes glanced out the window at the humanity teeming all around us.

"The rational versus the sacred, Watson . . . sometimes faith is stronger than reason. And perhaps that isn't entirely a bad thing after all. In a way, the Captain's belief in the ghost of his wife was a way of expressing his love and faith."

If I was startled at hearing my friend talk like this, I didn't say so; sometimes with Holmes it is best to listen and not interject one's own opinion. Moreover, I was afraid if I expressed my surprise at hearing him make such a statement, he would clam up entirely on the subject. So I just sat quietly and listened, but he said no more, and stared moodily out the window the rest of the way home.

The next day I called on Holmes to accompany him to the train station, from whence we would take a train to the Lake District. He was standing at the desk staring at that morning's paper, which had evidently just arrived.

"Holmes?" I said, but he did not reply. "Holmes?" I repeated. "Are you ready to go?"

"Oh, hello, Watson," he said, looking up at me, or rather past me, for his expression was preoccupied.

"Are you all right, Holmes?"

"What? Oh, yes, Watson, quite all right," he answered with a deep sigh.

"What is it, Holmes?"

He held up the paper. "The chickens have come home to roost, as they say. Or the vulture, rather."

I looked at the section he indicated. It was a small article in the bottom corner of page four.

MAN TRAMPLED UNDER CAB

Bystanders watched horrified yesterday as an intoxicated sailor lurched under the wheels of a speeding cab on Mary-Le-Bone Street yesterday. The man's identity has not yet been released, but witnesses say he was a sturdy red-haired man dressed as a sailor.

I looked at Holmes. "Snead?"

"No doubt. And I would lay odds that he wasn't drunk, and that it was no accident."

"Moriarty?"

Holmes nodded grimly. "Snead may have escaped drowning, but he was unfortunate enough to fail the Professor, and that is not wise if you wish to remain alive."

"But why would Moriarty have his own man killed?"

Holmes shrugged. "Who can say? To set an example, perhaps. Because he had outlived his usefulness, because he knew too much — who can say?"

I shuddered. I had no great affection for Snead, and did not doubt that he was a villain, but to be trampled to death — murdered by his own employer — surely that was too horrible a fate for anyone.

Holmes pulled back the curtain from the window and looked down into the street. "It is also possible that Moriarty intends to send me a message."

"You!" My blood ran cold in my veins.

"Surely Moriarty recognized my hand in this affair, and he is not finished with me. We shall hear from him again, no doubt."

"Holmes, how can you speak of such a threat — such a monster — so calmly?"

He shrugged. "What else am I to do? We are two players on the same board. He makes his move; I make mine. And so on. Sooner or later, one of us is bound to win. Until then, what can we do but continue to play the game?"

But I had enough of such talk.

"Holmes, let's go — we have a train to catch."

"Very well, Watson. I have agreed to come with you, but I don't want to put you in any danger, in case Moriarty is intent on exacting revenge upon me."

"Since when have I ever refused to face danger with you?" I said.

Holmes smiled. "Good old Watson, stalwart to the last. Come on, then," he said, laying a hand upon my shoulder. "Mrs Hudson has packed us a lunch, so we won't starve, at any rate."

With that, he picked up his suitcase and followed me out into the street, closing the door behind him. The sound of the closing latch echoed hollowly behind us as we walked down the stairs and out into the early morning glare, to be swallowed up into the sea of humanity that is London. ✗

Carole Buggé's short fiction has appeared in numerous anthologies. Her first Holmes novel, The Star of India, *received good reviews from* Kirkus, Publishers Weekly, Library Journal, The Boston Globe, *and* Ellery Queen Mystery Magazine, *among others; her second novel,* The Haunting of Torre Abbey, *received a coveted starred review in* Kirkus. *The 1992 Winner of the Eve of St. Agnes Poetry Award, she is also the 1996 First Prize winner of the Maxim Mazumdar Playwriting Competition and the 1992 Jean Paiva Memorial Fiction award, which included an NEA grant to read her fiction and poetry at Lincoln Center. Her play,* Strings, *has recently been optioned by The Open Book Theatre Company for a production in New York.*

The Mystery of the Missing Automaton

by Ron Goulart

On that rain-swept morning in May of 1900 only five automobiles existed in the capital city of the small middle European country of Orlandia. By the time Harry Challenge had been in town less than an hour the total was down to four.

His train came chuffing into the vast, chill South Gate Railroad Terminal roughly a half hour behind schedule. Harry, a lean clean shaved man in his early thirties, had been in Paris incapacitating a team of blackmailers who'd been plaguing Jules Verne. A cablegram from his father sent him to Orlandia.

The cable, now neatly folded in the breast pocket of his conservative dark business suit, said:

Dear Son:

Time to be up and going to Zevenburg, capital of dinky Orlandia. Colonel Milford Bascom, the circus entrepreneur, is in Europe gathering acts and artifacts for that halfwit Museum of Marvels here in Manhattan. He's in Orlandia to buy an automaton that plays the zither. However, the owner of the mechanism was murdered and the gadget swiped. We're hired to find it. Notify him of your arrival time and he'll meet your train. Your loving father, the Challenge International Detective Agency.

The rain was striking hard at the high glass-domed roof of the station. The platform was thick with disembarking passengers, bright-uniformed porters and a wide selection of portmanteaus, reticules, trunks, carpet bags and suitcases festooned with travel stickers.

Carrying his single piece of luggage, Harry stopped clear of his compartment and onto the platform. He set his suitcase down, fished a thin black cheroot out of his breast pocket and lit it with a wax match.

Nearby a small plump woman was mentioning to her small plump husband, "We had six pieces of baggage when we left Paris, Stanley."

"I thought it was only five, Marilyn my dear."

Exhaling smoke, Harry glanced around. Since he'd seen Colonel Bascom's picture on quite a few posters, he was certain he'd be able to spot him. So far, though, there was no sign of him.

"You're seriously late. I certainly hope this isn't a sample of the efficiency of your agency, Mr. Challenge."

Turning to his right, he saw a tall, darkhaired woman who was enclosed in a full-length black cloak. "Nope, it isn't, ma'am," he assured her. "Usually, when I see that my train is running late, I get the engineer to let me take over. Since I don't mind if I skip a station stop now and then or hit an occasional cow, I make much better —"

"Flippancy, I find, is not an excuse for inefficiency."

After a long careful puff on his cigar, he inquired, "Who are you?"

"I see that, in spite the bill of goods your father sold Colonel Bascom," the young woman said, "you haven't sufficiently familiarized yourself with the Colonel's various business enterprises."

"I regret that, yep," he said. "But when I only have a couple of days or so between cases, I find it curtails my research efforts terribly. Are you with the Colonel's freak show?"

Making a disdainful noise, she pulled open her cloak and spread her arms wide. She was clad in sparkling tights of an intense pink. "I happen to be Opal Archer, Queen of the Circus Aerialists."

Nearby Stanley gasped at the sight of the revealed young woman.

"Don't look," cautioned his wife.

"Yes, my dear."

Harry asked, "So where's Bascom?"

"At the hotel obviously," Opal Archer replied. "Surely you don't expect him to journey out in bad weather simply to greet an employee."

"Well, sir, I did yes," confided Harry. "Fact, I was also hoping for a bouquet of roses and possibly a fruit basket."

Scowling, the young woman shut her cloak. "If you're through making inane remarks, Mr. Challenge, I'll drive you to the hotel so you can start doing your job."

"Okay, and en route you can fill me in on this missing automaton and —"

"The automaton, known as Mme. Theresa, was built in 1835 here in Orlandia by that gifted technological craftsman Ogden Zimmerman. It soon gained fame all over the Continent and in America," she said, bending from the waist to grab up Harry's small black suitcase. "After a disastrous fire in the Zimmerman's workshop — that was nearly fifty years ago — the zither-playing mechanism was believed destroyed."

"But apparently it wasn't." He took the suitcase back from her and followed her along the terminal platform toward the exits.

"No, obviously. Two years ago the Mme. Theresa automaton, after being lost for close to a half century, mysteriously resurfaced. The present owner, who lived in a chateau near here, eventually decided to offer it for sale."

He pushed open one of the heavy glass and wrought-iron doors, stood aside and Opal Archer, pulling up the hood of her cloak, stepped out into the rain. "Then somebody killed the guy and made off with Theresa and her zither."

"The Colonel is counting on your being able to find it again, though, having seen you, I have my doubts," the acrobat said. "I left Colonel Bascom's horseless carriage in a side street near here." She went striding off along the wet sidewalk.

Catching up with her, Harry said, "I didn't know the Colonel brought his automobile to Europe with him."

She gave an annoyed sigh. "Obviously he did, Mr. Challenge," she said. "Or I wouldn't be able to drive you to the Ritz-Zauber Hotel."

The acrobat frowned back over her shoulder at Harry. "Do try not to dawdle," she called. "We're frightfully late as it is."

Harry had paused at the narrow window of a narrow curiosity shop. He was looking in at the scatter of artifacts on display. Sprawled amidst a clutter that included three ornate gilded music boxes, a glazed yellowish skull, a stuffed owl and a top hat were the rusted remains of what had once been a fortune telling automaton.

Nodding, Harry left the window and moved along.

The car, parked near an ornate lamp post, was glistening black in the rain. It was big and square, looking somewhat like an immense safe with windows and wheels.

"I have some parcels and items of luggage in the back seat," Opal Archer told him as she opened the front door on the passenger side. "You'll be obliged to seat yourself next to me."

As Harry started to enter the vehicle, she caught his arm.

"Goodness, I'm a fine one to criticize you about inefficiency," she confessed ruefully.

"How's that, ma'am?"

"I've just remembered that I left my handbag back at the pastry kiosk in the terminal."

"Describe it and I'll trot back to —"

"No, no, Mr. Challenge. I don't believe in making anyone run my errands for me. Just settle yourself in the automobile," she suggested. "I'll be back in no time." Turning on her heel, she started striding back along the route they'd come.

Shrugging, Harry climbed inside the car, shut the door. After glancing over into the backseat, he dropped his suitcase atop a large bulging canvas sack.

"Yikes!" exclaimed the sack.

Harry leaned over. "Beg pardon?"

"They knocked me for a loop," muttered a gruff, groggy voice. "How long have I been out cold, chum?"

"Well, it just struck eleven," Harry told the sack's occupant. "If you know when you were —"

"Holy Hannibal! The bomb's set to go off at five past eleven. I heard those rats plotting that during one of my spells of lucidity before they coldcocked me yet again."

"A bomb? Planted in this car?"

"You got it, pal. Not someplace in Egypt or North Dakota."

Harry jumped clear of the machine, hit the wet sidewalk and yanked open the rear door. He tugged out his suitcase and then the canvas sack, which was noticeably light.

Dropping the sack just beyond the lamp post, he loosened the drawstrings and took a look inside.

A very small man, dressed in a wrinkled suit of evening clothes, was scrunched up in there. "Save your gawking for a later date, rube," suggested the small man, "and help me get the hell out of this blinking sack." Twisting, turning, he managed to thrust up his white-gloved right hand.

Harry helped the midget get free. "Now let's get clear of the car." He grabbed up his suitcase in one hand, the small man by the back of his formal coat with the other, then started to run along the slippery street.

They'd covered less than ten feet toward safety when Harry slipped on the slick paving and fell, dropping both the suitcase and the midget. "A hell of a time to turn clumsy," complained the falling man.

As Harry went slamming into the ground, the horseless carriage exploded with a series of immense whumpings and thumpings.

Smoke, flame and shards of twisted black metal shot up and an intensely hot wind came chasing after them.

Harry pushed down with both hands, striving to rise. A large chunk of the automobile whacked him across the back of the head.

He dropped forward, but hit blackness before he hit the pavement.

"I thought that by this time, Harry, you wouldn't let a duplicitous woman lead you into an obvious trap. Especially one who is, in my opinion, not all that attractive."

Slowly Harry opened his eyes. "Now you've taken to nagging

me when I'm only partly conscious, Jennie," he said to the pretty auburn-haired reporter who was sitting in a fat purple armchair beside his bed. "You might've started off with some concerned questions as to how I feel or whether I'm on the brink of expiring from my wounds."

"You don't have any wounds, just a pretty big bump on your head," Jennie Barr assured him. "A mild concussion is all you're suffering from. I asked the doctor."

Harry, fully clothed except for his jacket and shoes, found himself lying atop an emerald green comforter in the middle of an ornately-carved four poster bed. "This isn't a hospital," he concluded.

"You're in a bedroom of Colonel Bascom's suite at the Ritz-Zauber," she told him. "He had you brought here from the Zevenburg Municipal Hospital. He and Major Nemo, that's the midget, will be barging in here momentarily. Soon as they realize you're awake."

"And why are you here in Orlandia? Has that yellow Manhattan newspaper you work for set you to dogging my trail again in hopes of coming up with another sensational story to entertain its vast readership of dolts and yahoos?"

"If you'd taken the time to read the cable I sent you at your Paris hotel, Harry, you'd know that I'm covering Colonel Bascom's European talent hunting tour for the Daily Inquirer."

"I never saw any —"

"And I suppose you never got the three letters I've sent you since we —"

"Okay, all right." With some effort, Harry sat up, lurched in Jennie's direction to take hold of her closest hand. "Excuse my surliness, Jen. Every time I get bonked on the skull with any portion of an exploding car, I tend to turn cranky," he said. "As to the letters, I got preoccupied with those smugglers in Sweden and then —"

"Sure, I know. Our trying to carry on any kind of romance is probably a —"

"No, it's possible. I'm the one who's at fault." Swinging his logs over the edge of the bed, Harry stood. He found that he had a tendency to sway a bit.

"Hey, the doctor suggested that you ought to lie quietly for a few more hours."

"Even so." He walked, very carefully, over to the window and looked down.

The suite was at least ten stories above the rainy street and the day had moved fairly close to twilight while he'd been unconscious. "Any idea why somebody wants to knock off both me and

Major Nemo?"

"There must be folks who don't want the Colonel to have that automaton."

"Can't be a rival miracle museum." He settled on the arm of her chair. "They rarely go in for murder."

"They want Mme. Theresa for some other reason."

"Yeah, we're going to have to find out why," he said, resting one hand on her slim shoulder. "That lady who was impersonating Opal Archer the noted acrobat — you implied you knew what she looked like and maybe who she is."

"Judging from Major Nemo's description, I'd bet that she's Perdita Molesworth."

Harry frowned. "Jonas Molesworth's daughter."

"That Perdita Molesworth, yes, Harry. Haven't you ever seen a picture of the lady?"

"Heard of her, never run across a likeness," he said. "Her father must be, after Professor Moriarty and Dr Grimshaw, the most notorious criminal mastermind in Europe. What the hell does he want with an automaton that plays the zither?"

"Theresa, obviously, has some other value that we don't yet know about," the reporter answered. "And, by the way, Molesworth has slipped some in the rankings. A piece in the London Times last month listed him as fifth most notorious."

Rising, Harry returned to the window. "I didn't get off to a very brilliant start on this damn case," he admitted. "Letting myself be hoodwinked by the opposition and then nearly blown up ... that doesn't make a very good impression on a client."

"Look on the bright side, Harry," advised Jennie, smiling. "You did save Major Nemo's life and Bascom's sure to appreciate that. After all, the major is a very valuable attraction."

"True, but still —"

There was an exuberant knocking on the door, followed by the entrance of a large portly man possessed of a great deal of white hair and mutton chop whiskers and a bright russet and gold checkered suit. He was followed by Major Nemo, who was decked out in an immaculate new suit of evening clothes.

Elbows resting comfortably on the crisp white tablecloth, Colonel Bascom studied the large, many-paged menu. "The Café Nirvana is one of my favorite restaurants on the continent, one of my best-loved eating establishments in all of Europe, a gourmet's haven to which I flock at every —"

"What the old duffer is trying to say is that he likes to eat at this joint," summed up Major Nemo, who was sitting on top of the first six volumes plus the eighth of the Encyclopedia Britannica as well as a carved wood chair.

"My diminutive Major," the showman explained to Harry, "has an unfortunate liking for terseness. As I was saying, Challenge, the Nirvana here is noted far and wide, from one corner of this giddy globe to the other, hither and yon as it were, for the exceptional breadth and international quality of its culinary offerings and —"

"I'm going to have a cheese sandwich and a beer." Nemo slapped his big menu shut, dropping it next to his assortment of gleaming silverware.

Far across the large, crowded restaurant, partially shielded by an assortment of potted palms, a string quartet was playing very subdued waltz music.

"Were you not impressively small, Nemo, were you not the epitome of littleness and an exemplar of midgetude, I'd have tossed you out on your keaster long since."

Harry asked the Colonel, "Any idea why Jonas Molesworth is after the automaton?"

"He isn't after it, Sherlock," put in the Major, "he's already got the blessed thing. The reason they tried to get rid of me while I was on the way to meet you at that drafty terminal was to prevent us from attempting to get that gadget away from them."

Shutting his menu, Bascom scowled. "How do you know that, my boy?"

"I heard them talking about it, Molesworth and that gawky offspring of his, while I was spending time in that blooming canvas sack."

Bascom tugged angrily at his white side whiskers, sighed with exasperation, leaned back in his chair and glared up at the glittering chandelier that hung high above in the domed, stained glass ceiling of the Café Nirvana. "I would have appreciated it, dear Major, if you'd seen fit to confide this information earlier."

"I'm telling you now."

Harry asked him, "What else did you hear?"

"Not that much, pal. They seemed to know when I came out of my stupor and they'd conk me again," replied Major Nemo. "But since your damned train was late, I was able to pick up some tidbits during my spells of wakefulness."

"Such as?" asked Harry, taking a sip of his white wine.

"Molesworth is absolutely not interested in zither music," said the Major. "Nope, they swiped Madam Tessie for another reason altogether."

"And that was?"

The Major gave a forlorn shrug. "If they mentioned the reason, Harry, it must have been during one of my unconscious periods."

"The automaton has been lost for a half a century," Harry reflected. "A hell of a lot could've happened to it in all those years. Could be Zimmerman hid something inside it or —"

"Flapdoodle," observed Nemo. "This isn't a Robert Louis Stevenson yarn, pal. I suppose you think there's also a treasure map involved in this rigmarole someplace?"

"The point to keep in mind," said Colonel Bascom, "is that I want very much to display Mme. Theresa in my New York museum. I've hired the Challenge International Detective Agency, at considerable expense, to find the automaton for me. Therefore, Major, cease insulting Challenge."

"Some sleuthhound this guy is," observed the Major, producing a disdainful noise. "Right after I met him he fell on his arse on the wet pavement, then got knocked silly with a stray hunk of horseless carriage. We are not impressed."

Harry grinned. "You're right, Major Nemo," he said. "I haven't done much that's impressive thus far. About my only accomplishment was saving your carcass and the more I think about that, I'm not sure that's much of an accomplishment."

"Gentlemen, let us cease squabbling and determine what we're going to have for dinner," suggested Bascom. "Thereafter, we can return to the problem of the missing automaton. I am, to be sure, extremely eager to obtain that technological masterpiece for my Manhattan museum. After all, its inventor, Ogden Zimmerman, was a veritable genius. However, a meal here at the Nirvana is equally important to me."

"So we hear," muttered Major Nemo.

"It's a pity Miss Barr was unable to join us, Challenge."

"She's probably off hunting for Tessie. The lady wants to find that automaton before our inept gumshoe does," suggested the Major. "That'll provide her with a scoop for her trashy newspaper."

"Tut tut, Nemo. One doesn't have to be any more perceptive than you to notice that Miss Barr and Challenge are close friends."

"A dame can be your close friend and still boot you in the fanny."

Colonel Bascom cleared his throat and said, "I believe I'll start with écrevisses au sauternes," he said. "Although I'm equally fond of poisson au rhum Guadeloupe."

A waiter, wearing a suit of tails that he'd either bought when he was much heavier or borrowed from a larger colleague, came hurrying up to their table. On the silver salver he was holding in his gloved right hand rested a pale blue envelope. "A message for

Mr. Challenge."

"He's the mope with the goose egg on his noggin," announced the midget, pointing.

"I'm Harry Challenge." He took the envelope off the tray.

"How's the écrevisses au sauternes tonight, Maurice?"

"Excellent as always, Colonel," replied the gaunt waiter. "I, for myself, would prefer the eels in green sauce to start." He kissed his finger tips, smacking his lips. "Superb tonight."

The note, written in a left-slanting script, said: Friend Harry: Once again I've succeeded and I can help you find it. I must, regrettably, ask for a fee of 2000 pfennigs. Sincerely yours, The One and Only Tuffanelli.

As he refolded the note and slid it back into the envelope, Harry asked, "Is a pfennig still worth five cents American?"

"Down to four," answered Colonel Bascom.

"We can afford that." He pushed back in his chair. "I'll be skipping dinner, Colonel Bascom."

The Zevenburg Arcade stood in a disreputable corner of the city and had added electricity since Harry visited it early in the previous year. A small, somewhat ramshackle imitation of the Crystal Palace in London, it was now brighter, gaudier and noisier than before.

Leaning casually against the metal and glass wall to the left of the entry way was a pale, pudgy man in a checkered suit that outshined Colonel Bascom's. "You, sir," he called to Harry, "strike me as a lad in need of female companionship. I am prepared, for an laughably modest fee, to introduce you to any sort of nubile maiden you might desire."

Harry halted. "Well, I sort of have my heart set on a woman who can play the zither."

"You wouldn't settle for a trombone?"

"Afraid not, alas." Grinning, Harry continued on into the amusement arcade.

Working his way through the modest crowd, he went past a fortuneteller's booth, a pastry kiosk that smelled strongly of cinnamon and almonds, a ring-toss stand that was doing no business and halted in front of a narrow shooting gallery.

A bearded young man in the uniform of a sailor in the Orlandian Navy was shooting at wooden ducks with a venerable air rifle. Above the stand stretched an oilcloth sign that proclaimed The One and Only Tuffanelli Shooting Gallery.

Tuffanelli himself, a short, bald man of about forty, was sitting on a stool at the left side of the counter. "Have to shut down for fifteen minutes, lad," he told the sailor. "Take this golliwog for a consolation prize."

"I had me heart set on the Black Forest beer mug," complained the young man.

"Try your luck again in fifteen minutes." Dropping free of the stool, he nodded at Harry. "Around back."

There were upwards of forty stuffed golliwog dolls lying in a tumbled heap against the lopsided back wall of the small shed that sat behind the shooting gallery. "I got them for a bargain price by buying in quantity," explained Tuffanelli as he settled onto one of the two bentwood chairs the room contained.

"What about the automaton?" asked Harry from the other chair.

"What about my 2000 pfennigs?"

Harry reached into the breast pocket of his coat for his wallet. "How's your sideline coming along?"

"This shooting gallery is my sideline, Harry," answered Tuffanelli. "Being the most trusted and respected informant in Sevenburg — indeed, in all of Orlandia — is my true calling."

"And are you thriving at your chosen profession?" Harry handed him four bright orange 500 pfennig bills.

"Actually my supplying you with inside information when you were working on a case here last year," explained the informant, "has helped a good deal, Harry. It's somewhat like providing wine to the palace. 'Official informant to the Challenge International Detective Agency.' Impresses prospective customers."

"Then I ought to get a discount."

"You are getting a discount," the bald man assured him, folding up the bank notes. "The man on the street I'd charge at least 3000 for this information."

"What exactly is it I'm buying?"

Leaning forward, lowering his voice, Tuffanelli said, "When you sent me that cable about your being on the trail of a zither-playing automaton, I immediately started keeping my ears open."

"What have you heard?"

"Zither music."

"Where?"

"Actually I didn't hear it myself," the informant continued. "But one of my many contacts, a fellow who imports brandy in an extremely unobtrusive manner, happened to pass the old Zimmerman Mansion that stands twenty miles beyond the city. Two nights ago this was and he saw lights burning when he passed — struck him as unusual for a house that's been deserted and shut down for many years. Moving carefully closer, he heard zither music from within. Mostly very old music hall tunes, he tells me."

"Did he notice anything else?"

"No, since he didn't think it wise to linger."

Harry asked, "The mansion once belonged to Ogden Zimmerman, the guy who built the automaton, didn't it?"

"No, actually it was his brother who last resided there. It's a grim old pile, especially with the Zimmerman family cemetery right smack next to it."

Harry straightened up. "The Zimmerman Emeralds," he recalled. "Yeah, they disappeared about the same time the automaton did."

Tuffanelli nodded. "There were those who believed back then that Ogden helped finance his automaton workshop with the profits he made from selling the jewels that he swiped from his family."

"If his lab burned down, and him with it, before he had a chance to fence the emeralds ..." Harry got to his feet.

"Be careful on this, Harry," warned the bald informant. "Jonas Molesworth is also interested in the automaton. That nasty daughter of his has already tried to do away with you, hasn't she?"

"An attempt was made, yeah," he said. "Can you tell me how to get out to the Zimmerman Mansion?"

"I surely can, Harry. And I won't charge you a single extra pfennig for the information."

Having tethered his rented roan mare in the woods that bordered the Zimmerman Mansion, Harry made his way on foot through the misty night toward the long-deserted old house.

The mansion, built of grey stone, was rich in spires, turrets and slanting slate roofs much in need of repair. Off at the mansion's left, at a distance of about a hundred yards, stretched the old Zimmerman family burying ground.

Light flickered behind three of the shuttered windows on the ground floor of the otherwise dark and shadowy house. Halting at the edge of the woodlands, shielded by high brush, Harry watched the place. He was about thirty feet from the front of the decrepit old house. With the mansion so in disrepair, it ought to be fairly easy to sneak in by way of a rear door.

Loud grating and creaking sounds came drifting to him. When the high, wide and heavy oaken front door came swinging open, a man and a woman emerged into the misty night. The woman looked very much like the spurious acrobat who'd waylaid him at the railroad terminal. She was clad in the same dark cloak, though her hair was now blonde. The man was short and wore a black suit and black beret.

His moustache was thick, waxed and curled up at the ends.

He looked very much like the photos of him that Harry had looked over at the State Police headquarters earlier in the evening.

Perdita Molesworth was carrying a shovel under her arm the way a hunter carries a rifle. Over his shoulder the elder Molesworth was toting a large canvas sack of the sort Major Nemo had spent part of his morning inside. Whoever was in this sack began to kick, squirm and give out muffled groans of protest.

From his coat pocket Jonas Molesworth yanked out a blackjack. Dropping the sack to the weedy overgrown lawn, he squatted and poked at it. Nodding, he brought down the blackjack on what was apparently the head of the captive within. The sack ceased its struggles.

Molesworth chuckled, hefted up the sack and tossed it over his shoulder.

His daughter, making an impatient gesture, started striding in the direction of the small family cemetery that lay to the left of the mansion.

Harry waited a moment, then, keeping at the edge of the forest, started following the pair of them.

A wrought-iron fence, leaning in a variety of directions and dappled with splotches of rust, surrounded the half acre of weed-infested ground that was the home of a dozen or so time-worn tombstones and a single marble crypt. The rusted gate, which hung half open on a single hinge, produced a harsh keening noise when Perdita yanked it completely to one side.

The mist was growing thicker as Harry left the protection of the trees and brush to head for the cemetery.

"Yet another example of my efficiency, dear child," Molesworth was saying while he and his daughter approached the ivy-encrusted crypt. "We dig up the long lost Zimmerman Emeralds and then deposit this unobtrusive female newshound in the resultant hole."

"If you were truly efficient, father," Perdita remarked, "you'd have solved the cipher etched on Mme. Theresa's backside long before this."

"Such work requires patience," he reminded in his tenor voice. "A quality that you and your late mother lack."

"And you wouldn't have wasted time getting the damned automaton to perform perfectly again," added Perdita. "Of all the unpleasant sounds of Earth, zither music is —"

"One of the qualities that lifts me above the pack of run-of-the-mill criminal masterminds is my dedication to perfection," he told her, dumping the sack in the high weeds to the right of the tomb.

On the roof of the crypt sat two small and very forlorn angels.

Between them hunched a carrion crow. When the sack thumped to the ground, the crow produced an annoyed squawk and took flight, soon swallowed by the surrounding mist.

Molesworth and Perdita continued on their way, circling behind the crypt.

Harry had been crouching behind a large, wide tombstone dedicated to the memory of Baron Egon Zimmerman (1780-1841) and topped by an angry angel brandishing a sword. He emerged now and, swiftly and quietly, made his way to the fallen canvas sack. Genuflecting next to it, he loosened the drawstrings at its mouth.

Inside, as he'd anticipated, was Jennie Barr. Bound and gagged, she was in the process of regaining consciousness.

With his pocket knife he cut the strands of greasy ropes around her wrists and ankles, then extracted the polka dot handkerchief that had been wadded up and thrust in her mouth.

"Your zeal," he whispered while rubbing her wrists, "has once again got you into —"

"Oh, hush up," the reporter suggested, sitting up. "I had a tip from one of my local informants that zither music had been heard hereabouts, so —"

"Would your informant be a guy who imports brandy in a somewhat unorthodox way?"

She nodded and, with his help, stood up. "The Zimmerman Emeralds were buried by Ogden in a gravesite behind this tomb. He etched, in cipher, the exact location of the jewels on the surface of the automaton and ...Harry, look out!"

He spun around in time to see Perdita, black cloak billowing out, charging toward him and swinging the shovel.

Harry backed against the marble wall of the crypt and dropped to a sitting position.

Carried forward by the force of her swing, Perdita stumbled and she and the shovel slammed into the wall. She fell and the shovel bounced away to land at Jennie's feet.

While Perdita was thus occupied, Harry yanked out his .38 revolver from his shoulder holster and shot the aggressive young woman in the thigh.

"How ungentlemanly," she muttered, toppling over sideways and passing out.

"See here, Challenge, you blackguard, I won't allow you to go around peppering my only daughter with bullets." Molesworth had come trotting around from the back of the crypt.

He was clutching a derringer in his right hand. Halting, spreading his legs wide, he aimed the tiny weapon directly at the crouching Harry.

Jennie, who'd grabbed up the fallen shovel, tossed it now at the tenor-voiced master criminal.

The blade hit him in the vicinity of the kidneys. Yowling in pain, Molesworth stumbled.

Harry, upright again, lunged and caught Molesworth's gun hand. He brought the arm down like the handle of a pump and the derringer's single shot dug into the weedy ground.

He then socked the criminal mastermind on the chin three times, hard.

Molesworth tottered, slumped, fell to the ground and stretched out beside his daughter on the hallowed ground, out cold.

"Despite your uncalled-for criticism of me," said Jennie, gathering up the strands of rope that had recently held her, "I do appreciate your saving me, Harry."

"I, too, appreciate my saving you," he told her, "since I'm quite fond of you." Leaning, he kissed her.

After a moment, Jennie said, "Okay, now let's wrap up these two and turn them over to the law."

While winding rope around Molesworth's ankles, Harry inquired, "Is Mme. Theresa inside the mansion?"

After binding up the leg wound with the polka dot handkerchief, Jennie was tying up the unconscious Perdita. "That she is," she said. "But I can't see why Colonel Bascom is so eager to display her. She really is a rather second rate musician."   ✗

————————————

Ron Goulart has been a professional writer ever since he left college at UC Berkeley several decades ago. He's written a lot of stuff in the mystery, science fiction and nonfiction areas. Twice he's been nominated for the MWA Edgar, once for the SFWA Nebula and once for the Will Eisner Award. His latest mystery novel is Groucho Marx, King of the Jungle *(2005) and his latest nonfiction work is* The Comic Book Encyclopedia *(2004).*

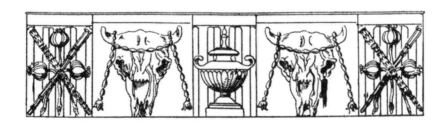

The Bet

by Marc Bilgrey

"**I**s this seat taken?" said a voice.

I looked up from the novel I was reading and saw a man who I knew to be one of the club's senior members staring down at me. "No," I replied, "no one's in the library but me."

"Very good," he said, and sat down on the wing back chair next to mine, holding a copy of the Wall Street Journal. Then he eyed me and said, "You're young Chester, aren't you?"

I admitted to it.

"Rollo Trundell," he said, nodding. "Your father and I used to see each other at the exchange quite often. Sorry to hear about his passing."

"Thank you. He was a good man."

"That he was," said Trundell, and opened up his newspaper. For a minute or two he didn't say anything and then he turned to me and said, "What're you wasting your time reading that trash for, young man?"

I shrugged and looked at my novel, then back at him. "Nothing like a good mystery to take your mind off the cares of the day."

"Trash, chewing gum for the eyes. What's the point of them? To find out who killed whom? Exercise in futility."

I wasn't used to having my choice of reading matter questioned, let alone impugned. "I happen to like to read a good crime story every now and then, sir. No harm in it."

"A good crime story? In this city there's enough of the real thing going on without having to read some half baked writer's idea of murder and mayhem."

Trundell was not a man I cared to have a row with so I decided to let him have his say and not allow myself to become agitated. "Mr. Trundell —"

"Rollo, please."

"Rollo, I appreciate your opinion on my choice of reading matter, but I must respectfully disagree."

"Your father was a stubborn man, too. I admire stubbornness. But, see here, this mystery business is really a crock. What useful purpose does reading all that rot do anyone? And don't tell me that it gets your mind off things. That's what women were invented for." He chuckled to himself.

I had no wish to offend Trundell, whose reputation for crudeness was, I now saw, well deserved; however, I did not feel like being the butt of his jibes, either. I debated getting up and leaving, but this option would certainly do nothing if not offend. Trundell was a legend on Wall Street and one never knew when a legend could be helpful to one's business. Better to make an ally than an enemy.

"Perhaps reading mysteries isn't the world's most productive way of passing a few hours," I conceded.

"Don't go turning into a panty waist now, Chester." He didn't ask my Christian name. "I liked you better when you were standing up for what you believe in. Even if what you believe in is a load of crap."

"Mysteries are not crap, sir."

He grabbed the book out of my hands and examined the back cover. "Jack Barnes committed the perfect crime but can he keep it that way?" he read. "The perfect crime!" he laughed. "Tell me what possible merit this junk could have in the real world?"

"Not everything has a practical application."

"Oh, please. The perfect crime, indeed. What nonsense."

He had my back up, but, as I say, what could I do? Insulting him had landed lesser men than myself in the kind of trouble that one does not need. Why have to worry about avoiding someone at a social occasion in the future? Or having a potential investor back away because one of the 'important people' has deemed you unworthy? So there I was, forced to defend my choice of leisure time diversion and in the process bring the wrath of Trundell down upon me, or back down and be thought a weakling.

"I actually think that the perfect crime goes on all the time," I said, surprised by my own words. Then, I realized, what I was doing, was attempting to move the subject away from crime novels and bring it into the area of crime itself, and hopefully segue into something innocuous. Rather like a hurricane that is downgraded to a tropical storm and then a breeze and finally moves out to sea.

"What do you mean that the perfect crime goes on all the time?" said Trundell, clearly intrigued.

"I just meant that fiction merely mirrors what goes on in society, that's all."

"You can't get rid of me that easily, young man. When you say the perfect crime, are you referring to murder?"

"I'm referring to all crime, and yes, I suppose murder fits on that list as well."

"You think that many murders go completely unsolved?"

"Yes, of course."

"I see," he said, stroking his chin. Then he said, "I would define the perfect crime as someone getting away with murder and then profiting from it."

"Interesting definition."

"Well, certainly. What good is killing someone if you can't make money on the thing?"

"This is an odd conversation," I said, in order to say something, though I was happy to finally get the subject off my choice of reading material.

There was a pause. Then Trundell said, "I happen to know that your business is in need of capital."

"Whose business is not?" I said, with a smile.

"Yes," replied Trundell, "but not everyone's business is being trounced by Japanese competition."

"How did you—?"

"I have my sources. Of course, if you had an extra thirty million to pump into resource and development, you could find that elusive computer chip before they do."

"It's not possible that you could know about that. That information is privileged—"

"No information is privileged to someone who knows how to get it."

I bowed my head and admitted that he had accurate intelligence. I wondered how he had gotten it. Then I realized that he hadn't stayed at the top of the game because he had gaps in his knowledge.

"So, young Chester," he said, "how much is thirty million dollars worth to you?"

"I'm not sure I follow your point, sir," I said.

He looked around the deserted room. Then he looked back at me. "What would you be willing to do for thirty million dollars?"

"Do? Are you making me some kind of offer?"

"Yes, but not the kind you think. Are you a betting man?"

"One can't be in business and not be, Mr. Trundell."

"Rollo. Though, I wasn't thinking of the indirect gambling that might be called business. I mean the real thing. Roulette, baccarat, blackjack."

"I can't say that those kind of games ever held much allure for me."

Trundell looked at the arm of his chair, then said in a lower voice, "Suppose I said that I would give you thirty million dollars under certain conditions."

"I'd ask what the conditions were, of course."

"Suppose I said that I would bet you thirty million dollars."

"To do what?"

"To do something that I propose."

"You have me intrigued, I won't deny it. Though, as you no doubt know, I could not at this time put up a matching sum."

"Obviously not. No, this would be a wager that would follow these terms: I would put up thirty million and you would put up, say, oh, fifty thousand dollars. So, if you win the bet, you take home thirty million, if you lose, I pocket fifty thousand."

"As seductive an offer as this seems, I would not want to think that I was taking advantage of you, Rollo."

Trundell's eyes slitted. "No one takes advantage of me. No one. This offer is made in the name of sport. To me the money is not the significant factor."

I swallowed. The legends about Trundell were all apparently true, I thought. His brashness, his eccentricities. His liquidity. "The obvious question of course—"

"Aside from what kind of fool am I—"

"I didn't mean to imply—"

He held up his hand. "You didn't. The question is, what would you and I have to do to win the money. Well, the answer comes from your book."

And I thought that I'd done such a masterful job of changing the subject!

"What I am proposing," said Trundell, "is that both of us try to commit the perfect crime."

"The perfect crime?" I said, hardly believing what I was hearing. The usual conversations I'd had at the club since becoming a full member a little less than a year ago involved boating, golf and upon occasion, women.

"You heard me correctly," said Trundell. "Whoever can commit the more perfect crime collects the thirty million, or in my case gets to keep it. If you lose, you're out fifty thousand. Now, as I stated before, I define the perfect crime as murder with profit. It doesn't even have to be a large profit, it just has to enrich you more than you were before you committed the crime. By enrich, I mean financially."

I sat quietly for a couple of moments. If this bet had been proposed by another man I would have laughed it off as some kind of sick practical joke. Only this bet was coming from Rollo Trundell. A man not known for jokes. A man who was known for shepherding two presidents into office. A man who lesser lights might have characterized as a captain of industry, though that trite phrase didn't even begin to describe his true stature. In another time he would have mixed with giants, now he quietly wielded what could only be described as (if one went in for melodrama) an empire. Trundell was as serious as a man could be. He was someone whose name never appeared on the lists of the wealthy and powerful. He owned the places where those lists were published and made damn sure his name was never on them.

My entire business depended on getting that thirty million, and, at the moment, there were no other offers. And to make matters worse, the deadline was a scant four weeks away and then the whole matter would be moot. If I failed to raise the necessary funds, my place in the world would be seriously diminished, as well as my standing amongst those who counted. I gave it some more thought, though it was quite clear that the decision had already been made.

When I turned to Trundell, he placed his newspaper on the small table next to him. "The perfect crime," I said, "murder with a profit."

"Yes," he replied. "A week from tonight we shall meet back here and exchange stories. And each of us must bring along documentation of the crime and evidence of the profit. In the event of a draw, the winner shall be determined by the one who has profited most from the endeavor. If I make a dollar on it and you, a dollar and a quarter, you are the winner. Now then, shall we seal the wager?"

I shook his hand. "Done," I said.

He smiled. It was the coldest smile I had ever seen.

The next day, I packed my wife off and sent her to our cottage in Maine for a week. The pretense I used was that I needed to entertain alone for business reasons. She didn't question it. When she was gone, I sent our driver home and took out the car.

As I drove up Park, I decided that I must have been a lunatic to accept such a preposterous bet. Me, who had demurred on cricket wagers at school and who never dropped more than a hundred dollars at Saratoga. But then my thoughts drifted back to the Japanese. Damn it all! I had made a deal with the devil, I decided, but having accepted it, I had to see it through. It did not matter that I had done it during a moment of weakness, that, had calmer heads prevailed, I would have gotten up and left. No, I had given my word and so had, for lack of a better description, my adversary, and now, what was done was done. I was bound to abide by the terms of our agreement.

I drove to the edge of the East River and got out. I stared into the polluted waters and wondered what I could do to uphold my side of the bet. I was no criminal. I abhorred violence. It was with great reluctance at school that I even taunted the lower classmen (much less pushed them) though it was expected of me. But now, to agree to murder, well, it went against the grain. Still, there was the matter of business. An infusion of such a sizeable amount of capital would not only save the company, it bore the very strong possibility of elevating it (and me along with it) to a strata never before known by my family. The company could quite possibly prosper beyond mere business, providing me an entree into the upper echelons of power.

I got back into my car and began driving again. Aimlessly, through the park, down Fifth, up Madison, down Lexington. I hoped that an idea would come to me. But none did.

Two days later, I was still without the slightest notion of who to murder and how to make a profit doing it. It occurred to me that I could pick up a bum off the street, a homeless man, and do away with him, but what would the profit be in that?

If I was going to do this thing, I had to do it right. I had to show up old Trundell, beat him at his own game. The thought entered my mind to kill someone and sell their body to some medical school. But then I realized that bodies are donated, as far as I knew, and not sold for profit. That sort of thing only went on in bad Victorian gothic novels.

Another day passed. I was nowhere closer to my goal. At nightfall I once again got into my car and began driving with no destination in mind. I hoped that the motion or the constant change of scene would somehow inspire me to come up with a solution to my problem. I had even brought along a gun that had come into my possession as part of the legacy of a relative. Since the gun was from the Second World War, I knew that it was untraceable. The weapon was in fine shape and in good working order. This had been proved by me, months earlier with a few test shots into a pillow, at my house in Connecticut.

But what good was a gun without a victim? The chances of finding the elusive victim I sought seemed to grow more distant with each passing hour. I thought about the murder mysteries I'd read. The kind of book that had gotten me into this conundrum to begin with. In those, people often took insurance out on their intended victim and then killed him or her. But there wasn't time to do that in this instance. And even if there had been, weren't there always very thorough investigations by the insurance companies in those sorts of cases? As much as I needed the cash infusion, I had no wish to be arrested and sent to prison.

Implied in Trundell's pact had been the proviso not to get caught. He didn't have to say it. How could one hope to use the ill gotten gains from a jail cell? It was an obvious footnote to the whole game. Kill someone, don't get sent to prison, make a profit. It had seemed like such a good idea at the club a few days earlier. I found it incredible that a single brandy had made me take such leave of my senses! But of course, I knew it wasn't the brandy that had done it. It was desperation. And fear. Two feelings that have toppled entire nations. And built them.

As I made my way around the dark city streets I decided to quiet my emotions. This, after all (I assured myself), was a business venture. No different than a merger or an acquisition. Looked at in that way, there could be no (or let us say, a minimum of) unpleasantness. But the problem remained. Who to murder? Certainly not anyone I knew personally. Though I could think of a few people whose death would not cause me to shed any tears, that was not the route to go. Besides, there was no money in it. At least not for me. And I had no wish to hasten the fortunes of the children of people I didn't care for. No, I would have to kill someone I didn't know. (Suicide had crossed my mind, as well, but what was the point? I would have to be at the club to collect in person.) A stranger would have to die. But who and how would I make a profit from it?

The streets were deserted now, as I continued my ride into the night. Perhaps, I thought, the key to the puzzle lay in assembling the pieces one at a time. First would be the who. Who would I murder? The answer came simply enough. A criminal. Someone who was a burden on society. Someone whom no one would miss. Someone who would be better off to the world, dead. Well, I said to myself, that solves the first part of the equation, now what about the second? Unfortunately I wasn't living in the old west, where they offered rewards for the capture of an outlaw, dead or alive. Besides, I reasoned, even if I had been, I didn't have the time to go looking for somebody who was wanted. I had a little problem with time.

At dawn I went home, happy to have solved at least half the problem. Some hours later, when I woke up, I was once again filled with anxiety. Sure, I thought, I could kill some criminal, but what good would it do if I couldn't fulfill the other part of the bet?

All through work I pondered the question. And then, as I was walking into my apartment that evening, the answer came to me in a flash. It was so simple that it had eluded me. The answer (like a DNA helix) was imbedded in the question. It had all started because I was reading a detective novel. The answer of how to murder someone and make it profitable was to kill your victim and then write a story about it and sell the story. It was truly the perfect crime.

Feeling a sense of confidence for the first time since leaving the club, I waited till dark and once again got into my car. This time I brought along an instant camera and my gun. I now knew, just as one can know that it will rain by feeling it in one's bones, I now knew that the money was mine.

At a little after midnight, I saw my victim. He was on a dark downtown side street. He was standing in the shadows talking with someone. Money exchanged hands, then a small clear plastic bag. The second man pocketed the bag and walked off. The first man was without doubt selling drugs. He would not be missed. In fact, I decided, that I was about to be performing a public service. It's amazing how the human mind can justify anything. I double parked my car halfway up the street and got out.

I took the gun out of my pocket and held it in my hand. It was hidden from view by my coat sleeve. If only more people would do things like this, I decided, then the streets would be safe to walk for women and children. The Scarlet Pimpernel, that's me. I took a deep breath then slowly approached my quarry.

He saw me and said, "Good smoke, man."

Without hesitation, I brought my arm up and shot him in the chest. He fell to the ground immediately. He started to get up and I shot him again. He lay motionless. I pulled out my camera and snapped his picture. Then I ran to my car and took off like a jet.

I was not followed. There were no police cars, no sirens, no flashing lights. And within minutes I was in another part of town. I disposed of the gun in the Hudson River, and then drove for another hour. Finally, I returned the car to my garage and then went back to my apartment.

I spent the remaining part of the night writing a story about a man who becomes a vigilante to rid his neighborhood of a local drug pusher. The description of the villain's murder was as I had done it.

The next day I called an old friend who was in publishing and told him that it was very important that I place a short story in one of the magazines that his company owned. I went on to tell him that the story was written by someone dear to me, under a pseudonym, and that I would consider it a favor to have it published. It would be a birthday present to that loved one. He (my friend) took it in stride and then asked me who the check should be made out to. I told him to make it out to cash. Then I asked him if it could be forwarded to me before the weekend. He laughed and said that if it meant that much to me he would make sure that it was delivered immediately. Then we talked about a rather sticky spot I had once pulled him out of (his wife never need know exactly what, thank you very much) and that was that.

"So," said Rollo Trundell, as he sat down on the chair next to mine at the library, "you certainly have a very self-satisfied smile on your face. Rather like the cat that ate the canary."

"I cannot deny it," I said, as I noticed, once again, that the room was deserted except for my companion and me.

"You have bested me, eh, lad?"

"That remains to be seen," I said, smugly.

"Those Japanese are going to beat a hasty retreat, eh?"

"One can only hope."

"Yes," said Trundell. "Well, then, let's get down to it, shall we? Please present your evidence."

I reached into my jacket and withdrew my short story and handed it to him.

"What's this?" he said.

"Read it."

"Who's Emily Rogue?"

"I am. It's my nom de plume."

"Hmmm," he said, eyeing me suspiciously. After he read the story, he handed it back to me. I placed it back into my pocket.

"Worst piece of garbage it's been my non-pleasure to read, but what's it got to do with our bet?"

"That piece of garbage, as you put it, is based on my perfect crime."

"How's that?"

"The drug pusher, the shooting, all real."

"You mean you—"

"That's right, down to the finest detail." Then I took out the photo I'd taken of the body and held it up so he could see it. "And here he is."

"I see," said Trundell. "Nice piece of work, but what has this got to do with—" That's when I pulled the check out of my pocket and handed it to him. "What's this," said Trundell, "a check made out to cash in the amount of four hundred dollars?"

"That's what I was paid for the story. It's going to appear in the fall issue of *Murder Mystery Magazine*. The perfect crime as set by your standards. A man is murdered. The killer is not caught and then profits from the crime." I sat back in my chair and smiled. Trundell looked at the check forlornly and then handed it back to me. "Well," I said, after a minute, "you seem awfully quiet."

"Just taking it all in, that's all," said Trundell, "just digesting it."

"Be careful you don't get indigestion," I said, smirking.

Then he smirked back. "You're not bad, young Chester."

"My name is John, Rollo."

"John? Yes, of course."

"Well, quit stalling, let's get to it, Rollo, shall we?"

Trundell's eyebrow went up. "Pride comes before a fall, boy."

I looked at my watch. "I haven't got all night."

Trundell stood up and walked to the bookshelves that lined the room. "Do you read the newspapers, young Chester?"

"Certainly," I said.

He turned around. "I mean besides the financial pages."

"Yes."

"That's good. It's important to keep up with the goings on in the world."

"But I don't see what—"

He interrupted me. "Do you read the international section of the paper?"

"Usually, yes."

"Perhaps you saw the international section of Friday's paper?"

"Yesterday? Yes, as a matter of fact, I did."

"Did you happen to see something about a place called Baranna?"

"Baranna? No, I must have missed that." What was he talking about? Was he trying to get out of the bet? Was it a ploy to change the subject and make me forget all about it? Just as I had tried to get the subject away from mysteries a week earlier. Could the great Rollo Trundell be trying to welsh?

"Baranna is a small country in Africa."

"Why should that concern me?"

"Ah," he said, "but it does concern you. Two days ago something happened in that tiny little country that affects you very much."

"What?"

"There was a civil war."

"So?"

"Five hundred people have been killed so far."

"And what—"

"I started that war this week. Oh, don't look at me so strangely. It's easy to start a war if you know the right people." He reached into his pocket and pulled out two small pieces of paper about the size of laundry tickets and handed them to me.

I looked at them. The papers had the numbers seven hundred thousand and Trundell's name written on them. Each had a different signature at the bottom.

"They're the bills of sale from both sides," said Trundell. "I sold them guns."

I stared at the two pieces of paper in my hand and then he reached over, took them back and put them into his pocket.

"The perfect crime," he said.

I felt my stomach go into knots. "B-but what are they fighting over?"

"The usual things, it's always the usual things." I stared at him glassy-eyed. He reached into his pocket and handed me a newspaper clipping, "Perhaps you'd like to read the details."

I stared at the article. It mentioned words like freedom and tyranny.

"Well, then, young Chester, I will expect your check for fifty thousand dollars on my desk on Monday morning. As I look at it, you've gotten a rather inexpensive little lesson in marine biology."

"Marine biology?"

"Yes. Just because you swim with sharks doesn't mean you are one." Rollo Trundell smiled and then said, "It's been fun. Be seeing you." With that he nodded his head and walked out of the room.

I sat in the chair for some time. Eventually, I tossed the article into the fireplace and staggered to the door.   ✗

———————————————

Marc Bilgrey has written short stories that have appeared in numerous anthologies. His novel, And Don't Forget To Rescue The Princess, *a humorous fantasy, has just been released from Five Star Publishing and is available in bookstores, or online at Amazon.com.*

The Automaton Museum
by Edward D. Hoch

Simon Ark and I had driven down the Jersey Turnpike on that bright Friday morning in early spring, ignoring the occasional drifts of melting snow from winter's last gasp a few days earlier. Presently we left the Turnpike and crossed the Delaware River into Philadelphia. The Drexel Museum was west of the city, not far from Bryn Mawr, a sturdy mansion built in another era for a wealthy developer whose fortune had outlasted his fame.

In these early years of the 21st century, Winston Drexel was viewed as something of an eccentric, a multi-millionaire who'd spent too much of his fortune building a collection of wind-up toys. He'd died back in the 1970s, leaving a will that stipulated his home be turned into a museum to house his collection of nearly a thousand elaborate music boxes and automatons dating back to the 16th century.

The museum had been under the care of his son Raymond until a few days ago, when he died under circumstances of the sort that caused people to seek out Simon Ark for help. "It appears he was killed by one of the museum's automatons," his daughter Meredith told Simon on the phone, "but the police are still investigating. I need your help."

So here we were, driving up to the Drexel Museum. "You're getting to be something of a private eye," I chided him, "when people phone you to investigate murders."

"I've done it all before," he reminded me. "And the idea of murder by automaton intrigues me."

Though Raymond Drexel's death had occurred four days earlier and the funeral had been held the previous morning, a single sheriff's car was still parked outside the front entrance of the mansion. I swung in behind it and we went up to the door where a simple sign announced: Museum Closed. There was a strong spring breeze blowing and Simon, in his usual black suit and billowing coat, looked a bit like a giant raven about to take flight.

An attractive young woman I took to be Meredith Drexel answered the door, closely followed by a grim-faced man with broad shoulders and a narrow necktie who could only have been a detective. "Mr. Ark, how good of you to come!" She held out both hands to accept his, seemingly unfazed by his withered features. Simon introduced me but I rated only a nod. "This is Sergeant

Collins from the sheriff's office," she added, sweeping her arm toward him. She was a great one for gestures, and I wondered if she might be an actress.

Collins came right to the point. "Are you a licensed private investigator, Mr. Ark?"

"No, merely a consultant."

"Certainly Miss Drexel is free to hire anyone she chooses, but you should know that our investigation is just about complete. Mr. Drexel's death was accidental."

"I'm not so sure," the young woman responded, eyes flashing in anger. "Suppose we show Mr. Ark the scene and see what he thinks. Let me take your coats, gentlemen."

Off to the side I could see a large parlor filled with display cases. A chicken was walking along the floor and paused briefly to lay an egg. "What's that?" I asked.

Meredith Drexel smiled. "It's one of our chickens. I was showing Sergeant Collins how it worked when you arrived."

"It's not real?"

"Clockwork, like just about everything in here. Back in the 18th century you wound them up. Today you'd use batteries for toys like these."

I shook my head in amazement and followed them upstairs. "This room was where he died," the detective explained, opening the double doors. The sight that greeted our eyes stopped me cold, though Simon stepped into the room as if he'd been expecting it all along. A row of six headless figures, not unlike tailor's dummies, lined one wall. Each of the iron figures had two great hooks for arms, and their bodies were painted in various colors. There was a small switch on the chest of each figure, and grooves in the floor to guide their progress about the room. The rest of the room was given over to bookshelves and a desk with two chairs.

"This room was my grandfather's pride," Meredith explained. "Each of these so-called servants performed a different task." She pushed the switch on the green figure and it immediately came to life, crossing the room on its grooved path to pick a book from the shelf with one of its hooked arms.

"Amazing!" I said.

Simon Ark smiled slightly. "I see that your grandfather was an admirer of Chesterton."

"What's that mean?" Sergeant Collins asked.

"Simply that this room is quite similar to one described in Chesterton's famous short story, 'The Invisible Man.' The victim in that story had a business, Smythe's Silent Service, supplying these automatons for domestic service as butlers and maids. In the story they were merely a red herring, having nothing to do with the solution."

"They're no red herring here," the detective informed us. "From all indications one of them cut into Raymond Drexel's throat with those hooked arms. His attorney found the body on the floor here by the desk. One of these robot things was still moving around the room aimlessly, with blood on its hooks."

"Which one?" Simon asked, studying each of the headless machines in turn as if he could discover the answer himself

"The red," Meredith answered. "My father had it set up to bring him a decanter of Scotch when the switch was pressed. He often talked of installing electronic gear that would respond to a remote signal like a TV set, but that would have involved corrupting the original 19th century mechanism of the automaton."

Simon turned to the detective. "You're convinced the killing was accidental?"

"No reason to think it wasn't. I came by to tell Miss Drexel that we're closing the case. Our lab report confirms it was her father's blood on that robot's hook."

"I wish you'd stop calling them robots," she told him. "That word wasn't coined until 1920 by Karel Capek. Every item in this museum is older than that. They're properly called automatons, a word in use since the early 17th century."

Sergeant Collins shrugged. "Call them what you like, Miss. It's your museum, now that your father's dead. I would suggest you don't try to operate any of these particular rob—automatons, though. They could be dangerous."

He left them and went back downstairs. Meredith walked to the window to watch him drive away. "I don't like that man," she said. "Now that he's gone perhaps I can speak frankly."

"By all means," Simon told her. "What is there about your father's death that roused your suspicions?"

"This museum was my father's life, Mr. Ark. He had examined and operated every clockwork device many times over. It's inconceivable that he could die in such an accident."

"Then we need the names of everyone who was here the day he died."

"That would be easy. The museum has been closed all month for some minor but much-needed renovations. Only a few people—" She paused, glancing around at the headless automatons as if she expected them to start moving at any moment. "Can we go downstairs and talk? This room—"

"I understand." We followed her down to the room where we'd seen the chicken. It was filled with every manner of gadget, from antique music boxes adorned with dancing ballerinas to singing birds and climbing monkeys.

"Do these things all work?" I asked her, touching a miniature peacock that immediately unfurled its tail feathers for me.

"Certainly! Each is equipped with an elaborate clockwork mechanism that can be wound with a key. Some run for only a few seconds. Others, like the servant automatons you saw upstairs, have springs that can function for thirty minutes and can be turned on and off."

"What's this one?" I asked, drawn to an apple from which a tiny mouse emerged.

"That's one of several items my grandfather purchased from the Anglo-Irish fantasy writer, Lord Dunsany."

Simon Ark snorted. "At times, Dunsany's own life seemed a fantasy. I was in London back in the 1930s when he shot two zebras on Piccadilly."

"You must be joking," I said.

"No, no! Dunsany was a big-game hunter who'd never bagged a zebra. A gentlemen's shoe shop was promoting itself with a carriage drawn by a pair of zebras. Lord Dunsany positioned himself on Piccadilly between Fortnum & Mason and Hatchards bookshop. When the zebras appeared, trotting down the avenue, he shot them both dead."

"You're a font of information, Mr. Ark."

"If you live as long as I have, you acquire a great deal of eccentric knowledge. But let us return to the matter at hand. Who was in a position to have killed your father, and what could the motive have been?"

"Of course there's his will, but everything was left to me." She glanced at her watch. "My lawyer, Mr. Fox, is due here in an hour. Meanwhile, there's Grotton. Tim Grotton, the museum's curator. He worked very closely with my father. He might have been the last person to see my father alive."

"Might have been?"

"He should be in the basement workroom. I'll summon him so you can hear it from his own lips." With another of her flourishes she spoke to him on the intercom.

While we waited, I examined some of the other objects on the main floor, feeling like a child in a toy store. On one music box the figure of a magician removed his own head while some eerie tune tinkled away. Who were these people that collected things like music boxes and doorknobs and buttons? Eccentrics, surely — but were they any more eccentric than my friend Simon Ark?

Tim Grotton could probably be called an eccentric, too, or

perhaps merely a nerd in the vocabulary of today's youth. He was a tall angular fellow around thirty, with glasses that he wore on a cord around his neck. He spoke slowly and carefully, as if overcoming a possible speech impediment. "I—Meredith said you wanted to see me."

He'd addressed his words to me because I was closest to the door, but it was Simon who answered him. "I understand you were the last person to see Raymond Meredith alive, sir."

"The last unless someone killed him. He had some questions about last month's invoices and I explained them to him. I was with him perhaps twenty minutes or so."

"In the upstairs room where he was found?"

He nodded. "Mr. Meredith used that as his office. He liked to play around with those automaton servants in his spare time."

"Were any of them in operation at the time you were there?"

"Oh no, they were all against the—the wall in their rest positions."

"So far as you know, did he keep the clockwork mechanisms tightly wound?"

"Always! We have tours for schoolchildren who like to handle everything, and I have to go around and wind them all up again after they leave."

"Are the children ever allowed in the upstairs room?"

Grotton shook his head. "He always said it was too dangerous. The servant automatons moved all over the room, and school kids were too hard to control. That's why he used the room as an office and only showed it to special visitors. But I kept those servant automatons wound up for him, too."

"What time did you finish your meeting with him?"

He thought about it. "It must have been around ten-thirty because I remember him commenting that he had only a half-hour before his lawyer arrived at eleven."

"Were the automatons turned on when you left him?"

"No, he never had them on when h—he was working. He might have turned them on while he waited for Arthur Fox to arrive. That's his lawyer."

Meredith Drexel interrupted at this point. "Tell Mr. Ark what you told me, Tim."

He hesitated and then said, "Your father said he was thinking of selling the place." He actually lowered his voice when he said it, as if he feared the automatons might hear him.

She smiled slightly. "Sometimes he acted as if they were real people, or real animals. Once I found him trying to feed a cracker to the parrot, though he claimed he was only joking."

"So those iron torsos upstairs, with their hook-like hands, might have had a reason for wanting him dead," Simon mused, half to himself

"They move along grooves in the floor," Meredith reminded him. "And they don't have brains. My father could easily have avoided them."

"Monday would have been the morning of our last snow. Strange things happen in cold snaps. During the 16th to the 18th centuries, European records show there were more witch trials during years of cold weather."

I'd never heard that one before. "Maybe they needed to burn them at the stake to keep warm," I suggested, drawing a reproachful glance from Simon.

Our conversation was interrupted by the arrival of Arthur Fox. The tall balding lawyer had the glum expression of a funeral director, and when Meredith introduced us he asked, "Are these prospective buyers?"

"No, no," she assured him. "Mr. Ark is an investigator. I knew nothing of my father's interest in selling this place until Tim mentioned it to me. Do you think he was serious?"

"He sounded serious to me. He requested that I draw up a statement of the collection's value, based on an inventory he'd done two years ago. My personal opinion was that selling would be foolish. The things he has here are treasures, far more valuable than mere antiques. They can only appreciate in value."

"I understand it was you who found his body," Simon said. "Could you describe the scene as it was when you arrived?"

"Certainly."

"It might help if we go upstairs so you can indicate the exact position of the body."

"You go ahead," Meredith said. "Tim and I have some work to do here."

Arthur Fox led the way to the upstairs office. "Did you let yourself in on Monday?" Simon asked.

"Of course. I've been coming here for years. Usually the museum is open to the public. Right now they're doing renovations, but they left the front door unlocked."

"So anyone could have come in?" Simon asked.

"I suppose so, but they would have gone to Meredith's office or one of the other ground floor rooms. The only reason for going upstairs would be to see Raymond Drexel."

"And that's what you did."

"That's what I did. I could hear the automaton moving before I opened his office door." He pointed to a spot next to Drexel's desk, by one of the sunken tracks the automaton followed. "He was lying on his back about here, bleeding from the throat wound. That red server automaton was running along its track, carrying a tray between its hooked arms."

"What did you do?"

"I ran downstairs to get Meredith and Tim."

"Was the robot still moving?" I asked.

Arthur Fox smiled slightly. "She and her father never referred to them as robots. But yes, it was still moving. I wasn't going to touch it. When Meredith came upstairs she immediately turned off the switch and returned it to its wall station. When she removed the tray we saw the blood on one of its hooks."

Simon Ark strode over to the red metal automaton and placed his hand carefully on its chest. "I need to see this device in operation. Is this the switch?"

"Yes, but we'd better get Meredith up here to turn it on. She doesn't like anyone fooling with it."

He went to call her while Simon examined the automaton more carefully. "I assume this keyhole in the back is for winding. I wonder where the key is kept."

"When do you think something like this was built, and by whom?" I asked.

"Well, chess-playing machines were known in the early 19th century, although sometimes they had a little man hidden inside. There is even a story by Ambrose Bierce, 'Moxon's Master,' in which a clockwork chess machine kills its inventor after losing a game. I wonder—"

Meredith Drexel joined them and finished his thought. "You wonder if there's a midget or something hidden in here? I assure you there isn't. If we took it apart you'd see it was full of gears and tightly-coiled springs."

"Has it been rewound since your father's death?"

"No. I have the only key downstairs. When Tim rewinds them he must get the key from me. We haven't even thought of it since what happened Monday."

"Could you start it for us now? The red one, the one that—"

"Certainly." She reached up and pushed the little switch, as someone might turn on a light. Immediately we heard the humming of gears and she stepped out of the way as the automaton sprang to life. It moved forward on its track, then took a turn on a spur that ran to a liquor cabinet against one wall. "He often had a decanter of scotch and two glasses on that silver tray. The automaton lifted the tray and carried it over to his desk. It was geared to perform that action first every time it was turned on."

Simon and I watched intently as the red iron figure reached the cabinet, lowered its hooked arms and grasped the handles of the tray. Then it turned and retraced its route along the sunken rail, taking the path that led to the desk. There it lowered the tray, setting it gently on the desktop.

"Each of the five automatons is set up to perform different tasks. One is able to sweep the floor, another to pick up small objects. The green one can lift books from the shelves, as you saw earlier."

Having completed its assigned task, the red machine seemed to wander aimlessly, followed the course of the other tracks in the room. "It'll do that until its springs wind down, unless someone turns it off and wheels it back to the wall."

Simon frowned, adding to the permanent creases on his face. "In that Bierce story I mentioned, the chess automaton is driven to strangle its inventor because it is left running with nothing to do. Perhaps that is what happened here."

"I doubt it," the young woman replied.

"Why don't they have heads and faces?" I asked. It seemed a logical question.

"They were patterned after the clockwork serving machines Chesterton created for his 'Invisible Man' story. Some critics believe Chesterton was making a statement about how the upper classes looked upon their servants, like faceless machines with no individuality."

"Is it possible the machine might have killed him, like that chess machine in Bierce's story?"

But Simon would not accept that. "I will consider fancy only after fact has fled the scene. That time is not yet, not so long as this machine before us stays in motion."

Meredith thought about that, her eyes never leaving the seemingly aimless paths of the automaton. "I told you we've been officially closed for remodeling. My father and Tim and I were the only ones in the building until Mr. Fox arrived to find the body."

"Did you say your meeting with Drexel ended around ten-thirty?" Simon asked Tim Grotton.

"I've been all over this with the police," he answered. "I went up to his office a little after ten to explain some invoices. That's when he told me he was thinking of selling the museum and needed to get our financial records in order. He mentioned that Mr. Fox was coming out at eleven for that same purpose."

"Correct," Fox agreed.

"We talked for maybe twenty minutes. I came back down to Meredith's office at about ten-thirty."

She nodded. "Maybe twenty-five to eleven."

"And the automatons were turned off then?"

"That's right. He never had them on when I was up there on business. They were something for his own amusement and to show off to guests."

Simon turned to the lawyer. "Had you ever seen them in operation, Mr. Fox?"

"Before today? I suppose he showed them off the first time I was ever out here, some years back."

"And they were going today when you arrived?"

"Just the red one. The others were all at rest."

"So sometime between ten-thirty and eleven o'clock either Raymond Drexel or his killer turned it on."

Meredith spoke up. "When you put it that way, it had to be my father. Tim was downstairs with me for that entire half-hour. And the automaton was already in motion when Mr. Fox arrived."

"You're overlooking two possibilities, Miss Drexel. Tim might had done the deed before he left your father—"

"That's not true!" he objected.

"—or Mr. Fox here might have done it after he arrived."

"I'd have had no time," the lawyer objected. "I was down in her office by three minutes after eleven."

"But there's no one to say you didn't arrive a few minutes early. You would have walked right in the unlocked door, as you did today."

And then something unexpected happened. The red automaton with its hooked hands stopped moving, coming to a halt on the far side of the room. "It needs to be rewound," Meredith Drexel said.

Simon consulted his watch. "Twenty-three minutes since you started him."

"What does the time mean?"

"It means we should call Sergeant Collins back here and put an end to this."

He was there within the hour, joining them in the upstairs office where Simon Ark was holding court. "Do you have new evidence?" he asked. "Something to verify that the death was accidental?"

"It was not accidental," Simon told him, seated behind the desk where Dexter had sat the morning he died. "That was obvious to me from the beginning. We all saw how the automaton operates. You push the switch and it comes alive, moving along the track to the liquor cabinet. There it picks up the tray with its hooks and brings it to this desk. It was here that Drexel's body was found, remember."

"And this robot had Drexel's blood on its hook."

"Exactly, Sergeant. But how could that hook have inflicted the fatal wound if it was holding a silver tray at the time?"

He had an answer for that. "It happened before the robot picked up the tray."

"No, because Drexel's body was by this desk, and the automaton never approached the desk until after it went for the tray. We're not dealing with a human mind here, Sergeant. It's a clockwork machine, with no power to change the operation it was built to perform. The killer inflicted the fatal wound, then smeared some of the dead man's blood on the automaton's hooked hand, pushing the switch to start the mechanism as he left the room."

"Tim Grotton!" the lawyer said, pointing an accusing finger.

"I didn't—," the young man began.

"You didn't," Simon agreed, "for two reasons. It was mentioned shortly after our arrival that the automatons in this room could only run for thirty minutes without rewinding. Yet you left your meeting with Drexel at 10:30 or 10:35. That meant the automaton, if fully wound at the start, had been running for about twenty-five minutes when Mr. Fox here arrived for his 11:00 meeting. You turned off the switch within minutes of that, Miss Drexel, but the mechanism still would have been nearly run down. You told us no one had rewound them, that you had the only key. Yet just now it ran for twenty-three minutes before running down. That means it had only been running about seven minutes when you came up here, found your father's body and turned it off. Since Tim was with you all that time, he couldn't have started it. Only you, Mr. Fox, could have done it."

"That's preposterous!" the lawyer fumed.

"Is it? In order to smear Drexel's blood on that hook and implicate the automaton, the killer had to be someone not familiar with the device's operation, someone who didn't know it went to pick up the tray before approaching the desk. Certainly Miss Drexel and Mr. Grotton here both knew exactly how the thing operated, but you admitted you'd seen it in motion only once, years ago. When you turned it on as you left the room, you had no idea of the route it must follow, no idea that the blood-stained hook would be picking up that tray."

"Why would I kill him?" Fox demanded. "What motive did I have?"

"I think Mr. Drexel's announcement that he might sell the

museum was motive enough. I suggest, Sergeant, that you have someone examine the museum's financial records. Drexel was questioning Grotton here about invoices, and I suspect he'd also found some irregularities to question you about, Mr. Fox. You knew with him dead the museum would pass to Meredith and any financial irregularities could be corrected over time."

Arthur Fox slumped in his chair, still shaking his head but saying nothing. He was too smart a lawyer to make a confession on the spot, but I could see the resistance draining out of him.

Some time later, as we were leaving, Meredith Drexel asked Simon, "Is there one of our small automatons you'd like as a remembrance? I feel I owe you something for what you've done."

Simon Ark looked around at the clockwork dreams of men long gone, men we'd never known. "Perhaps this magician who removes his own head," he decided. "I believe its maker must have been a kindred spirit."   ✗

Edward D. Hoch was a past president of Mystery Writers of America and winner of its Edgar and Grand Master Awards. He published over 950 short stories and several collections, most recently More Things Impossible *(Crippen & Landru).*

Moving?

Don't forget to take us to your new pad! Mail in your address changes to:

Wildside Press LLC
Attn: SHMM Subscription Dept.
9710 Traville Gateway Dr. #234
Rockville, MD 20850

Or email your changes
of address to:

<wildsidepress@yahoo.com>

ON THE HEIR
by Hal Charles

Kelly Locke rushed out of Makeup. 5:55. Only five minutes till air-time. Settling behind the too-too contemporary chrome-and-imitation-marble desk that dominated the NewsTeam 4 "Were Here Four You" set, she sensed the familiar butterflies unsettling her stomach. Even after one year as the co-anchor on the city's highest-rated news program, the pressure to perform was as palpable as the heat and glare from the bright lights. Inserting her wireless earpiece in her right ear, she covered it with her Katie-Couric-length auburn hair. Not much time to punch up her script before the red light for *The Six O'Clock Report* winked at her.

"Kelly, sweetheart," called an out-of-breath, raspy voice from the door to Studio A, "I'm so glad I caught you before you went on the air."

Expecting her ever-last-minute co-anchor Chuck Mann, she was caught off-guard by the bear-like figure lumbering in. Her father, Matthew Locke, the city's Chief of Detectives.

"My favorite source got a hot tip to heat up a cold news day?" she said, smiling. Her father's sudden appearances in her life usually meant a scoop or a plea for help on one of his cases.

"I brought you a gift," he said, still panting, and he handed her a plastic bag.

"You need help again, don't you?"

"Can't a father just bring a nice present to his favorite daughter without being treated to *60 Minutes*-style ambush journalism?" He kissed her on her right cheek, totally wrecking what Marie in makeup had thought of as her personal Sistine Chapel.

"Four minutes to air-time," boomed Stanley, her director, through the studio speaker. "And get Marie in here . . . quick."

"Dad, I don't have time to —"

"Open it," he said, sitting beside her in Chuck's empty chair.

Rather than argue, she reached into the Gifford's Rare Books and Collectibles bag and pulled out a dusty tome bound in red leather. "*The Adventures of Sherlock Holmes*," she read. "London, 1890. It's a fake. His first twelve adventures weren't collected until 1892."

"Of course, it's a fake, sweetheart. I wouldn't try to slip something so obvious by a true Holmesophile, a woman who's been reading the Great Detective's adventures since she was a little girl. You can add it to your collection of famous phonies."

Kelly shook her head. "O.K., Dad, what do you really want?"

"Am I that transparent? This'll just take—"

"Three minutes," bellowed Stanley. "Where's our Michaelangelo of makeup artists?"

Just then a tiny woman with Coke-bottle glasses and a makeup case bolted onto the set. She spun the anchorwoman's chair around and began dabbing powder in strategic places.

"About a year ago," said her father, "I established this CI in Reuben King's organization who's been feeding us information on a regular basis."

"CI?" said Marie, turning to look at Chief of Detectives Locke and inserting powder in Kelly's right ear.

"Confidential Informant," responded the cop. "Code name 'Egghead.' Last week he told me he had a feeling something new big was about to go down."

Kelly opened her mouth, but Marie clamped it shut and began to apply another coat of Sassy Cinnamon, Kelly's favorite.

"Every Tuesday," continued her father, "Egghead and I meet in rotating places. This morning he didn't show in the waiting room of the bus station."

"I was there last weekend," said Marie. "My sister from Saskatchewan—"

"Isn't it kind of risky for a CI to talk directly to you rather than one of your detectives?" posed Kelly.

"A few years ago I got Egghead out of a real jam-up when he was charged with forgery, so I'm the only one he'll talk to."

"Two minutes. Clear the set," ordered Stanley. "And where the hell is my prima donna anchorman?"

"Anyway," said her father, "I figured something had happened to Egghead. Then this afternoon I get an email from my nephew Edgar."

"But, Dad," protested Kelly, turning abruptly and catching Marie's powder puff like a beanball between the eyes, "I don't remember a cousin Edgar."

"That's because you don't have one. My guess is my informant was right. Something *is* going down very soon, but Reuben King runs a tight ship. Egghead couldn't shake free to contact me in the usual way, but he's a smart cookie and—"

"One minute," the director reminded her. "Miss Locke, far be it from me to disturb a family reunion right out of reality TV, but I must remind you there are some three-million viewers out there waiting for you like some contemporary watchman to assure them that's it's six o'clock and all's well with their world."

"Dad," said Kelly as Marie made a final swipe at her nose, "you've got to leave the set."

"Of course, sweetheart. As soon as I finish this."

"But . . . all right . . . if you have the email, what's the problem?"

"Thirty seconds," bellowed the director.

"Stanley," protested Kelly, "it's important—"

"Don't go diva on me, Miss Locke," returned her director. "If I have to come in there and throw that muscular male out on his heiny—"

"Heiny, my butt," said the Chief of Detectives, showing the first sign he was aware of the situation in the studio.

"Dad, please," begged Kelly.

"Ten seconds, your highness," thundered Stanley like an angry Norse god.

"The email," explained her father, "is a bunch of gibberish as far as I'm concerned. That's why I need your—"

Kelly's left hand shot out, pushing her father down behind the anchor desk just as the cameraman on One pointed at her and the red light flashed on above the equipment. "This is *The Six O'Clock Report*, and I'm Kelly Locke . . . on top of the news," she ad-libbed. "Chuck Mann is on assignment." Either suing his plastic surgeon, she thought, or offering the blonde summer intern one of Chuck's Tips for Breaking Into the Business. "Tonight's Top Story contains a note of sadness. Now that the Barons have moved from Homer Black Field to their new complex, the City Council has just sold the old ballpark to an unknown buyer. For a bit of nostalgia, we go to a live InstaCam report from Brian Fardo."

As the solitary reporter on a bridge overlooking the deserted field began his stand-up, Kelly turned away from the narration on her monitor. The red digital clock on the wall above Camera One told her she had 57 seconds left to get rid of her father.

"Dad, can this wait till 6:30?" she pleaded to the uncomfortable figure scrunched between the desk and the MaxTronic WeatherMation CompuMap.

"The game's afoot, Sherlocka. By 6:30, for all I know, King's boys could have pulled off the crime of the century — a heist, smuggling, a major hit, drugs. Of course, if you don't want to scoop Channel Seven's Action News . . ."

"Ooh, you know they're all 'If it bleeds, it leads'," she snapped back. Out of the corner of her eye she caught the short, scarecrow figure of Stanley entering the studio under the ON THE AIR sign. Surely he didn't intend to make good on his threat.

Suddenly Camera Two's light flashed. "Thank you, Brian Fardo, for that report," Kelly heard herself say. A piece of paper from off-camera appeared in her hand. Taking what she thought must be a news bulletin brought in by her director, she began to read, "Dear Uncle Matt . . ."

Clearing her throat, she turned back to Camera One. "That story coming up, but first." She read the teleprompter's piece on a local congressman defending his recent junket to Hawaii as necessary to his ongoing investigation of excessive sugar in his constituents' diets. Then she broke for a commercial.

"Dad," she exclaimed in exasperation, "are you trying to get me fired?"

"Fired up," said Matthew Locke. "Just finish the email."

One hundred and forty-six seconds to go. Kelly quickly scanned the email her father had labeled "gibberish."

Dear Uncle Matt,

As you requested, I have researched our friend's familial activity. He is indeed in line for a sudden windfall as befits his royal station.

By an act of Parliament in 1759, his regal ancestor was commissioned Viceroy for the court at Cambridge. What's more, it is true he sailed for Newport with the Duke of Kent on Christmas Eve.

His triumph is revealed in the family crest: a lion crouching beneath a rising sun on an empty field of sable.

Your nephew,
Edgar

The light on Camera Two flared red as Matthew Locke shot up like an errant jack-in-the-box. Just as suddenly Kelly shoved him back down.

"Back to the news," Kelly said. Then she read a puff piece about how lawyers for DJ Colin Oskopee would appeal the rap group's conviction at a recent Christmas concert for starting a riot by biting off the heads of three French hens, two turtle doves, and a partridge in a pear tree. All the while her mind busily sorted out the details in the email. It was starting to make sense.

Turning to Camera One, she said to a grinning man standing in front of a blue screen that her monitor electronically transformed into the MaxTronic WeatherMation CompuMap, "And what does the New Year hold for us weather-wise, Bill Frost?"

"There's no such word as 'weather-wise'," whispered her father from the bowels of the anchor desk.

Avoiding his criticism, Kelly whispered back. "Your Egghead is no dummy. He knew that Reuben King was reading his emails. I'll bet he still makes his living as a forger, and he contacted you on your personal email at home."

"Yes, he's an expert in faking documents to 'prove' families are descended from royalty . . . if the price is right."

"This isn't 'gibberish,' but a clever code disguised to look like he's been researching a family history for a client. Look at the first paragraph. He says, 'As you requested' — you asked him what King's mob was up to, and he's replying as to their 'activity.' And, as you suspected, King — remember 'his royal station'? — will make lots of money — soon."

"I'll buy that," bellowed the Chief of Detectives, forgetting to whisper and causing the weatherman to lose his concentration.

"I can't quite figure out the second paragraph, but the description of the family crest tells us something about the crime they're going to pull off, their 'triumph'."

Her father looked at her blankly while the weatherman droned on about the influence of Canadian lows and Mexican highs.

"The lion in the crest is the king of beasts," posed Kelly, "so Reuben King will commit the crime at dawn, as indicated by the rising sun."

"But where?" said her father, excitedly throwing his hands into the air and smashing the MaxTronic WeatherMation CompuMap at a spot just east of Houston.

As Bill Frost tried to explain the unexpected storm in the Gulf of Mexico, Kelly continued, "Sable is a term in heraldry for the color black. A dark field at sunrise."

"Dark? Deserted? Black?" said the Chief of Detectives. "That could be anywhere."

"Of course — Brian's story," she blurted out. "Somebody found a use for that abandoned stadium. But what crime could Reuben King be planning at a deserted Homer Black Field? The answer has to be in the second paragraph."

"Hmm," mused her father, firing up his curved pipe.

"Dad," protested Kelly, picturing a fuming Stanley, "there's no smoking on the set. Wait a minute!" Hastily she started circling key words in the second and third paragraph of the email. "It's elementary, my dear father," she said in her best Victorian accent. Then she read the encircled words. "Parliament, Viceroy, Cambridge, More, True, Newport, Kent, Eve, Now, Triumph, Merit. What do these words have in common?"

"They may have been banned from advertising on TV about the time you were born," said the Chief of Detectives, puffing on his pipe, "but they're still cigarette brands."

"King must be doing something illegal with cigarettes."

"Bootlegging. He buys them cheap in the South and trucks them up here. He has to have a place to store them before selling them privately to avoid the cigarette tax. What better place than deserted locker rooms?"

"King," Kelly concluded, "is the unknown buyer of the old ball-park."

"Who will be quite known tomorrow morning after my men are there when his trucks arrive at dawn." Matthew Locke grabbed his daughter and hugged her as weatherman Bill Frost tried to explain the strange cloud of smoke that had drifted up from the South. "Sweetheart, for Sherlock Holmes Irene Adler may have been the woman, but for me, *you* are the woman." ✗

———————

"Hal Charles" is the writing team of Hal Blythe and Charlie Sweet, two mild-mannered English professors in sleepy little Richmond, Kentucky. A collection of their short stories, Bloody Ground, *appeared from the Jesse Stuart Foundation a couple of years ago.*

Oh, come now, my dear — it's not like it's poison!

LOST AND FOUND
by Jean Paiva

"Really, Patti, you've done some crazy things before, but this takes the cake."

"Marsha, you've got to remember to call me Trish now. Patti is another person from another time and I'd just as soon forget her."

"That's another one of your insanities, changing your name at your age, but I'll try to humor you."

"And that's what best friends are best at," answered Marsha who was, in fact not only my best friend but perhaps my only friend.

After a divorce you can finally find out who your friends really are and after mine I found out. The neighbors sided with Ted and my co-workers probably would have if they had known him. He was charming and, as an athletic six-footer, managed to get on every committee that had a spot — that is, if the committee name sounded prestigious enough and didn't require too much real work. Meetings once a month were permissible, especially if it meant one less evening he had to stay home. The Community Planning Board, the Citizens for Better Schools, the Neighborhood Environmental Society, the Little Theatre at the Library and half a dozen others kept him out of the house evenings the equivalent of two weeks each month. He spent another week's worth of evenings playing squash at the club — excuse me — his club. The final week of each month was allocated for either going to neighbors' homes for dinner or cards, or having them over to our house, the latter the only activity that definitely included me.

Ted did lead an active life. My life involved coming home from work — a job we planned for me to quit as soon as our furniture and car were paid for and Ted's bills for his clothes and sports equipment was under control — and to sit in front of the television.

I barely saw him. There were, of course, mornings when, bleary eyed, both of us could look at each other from behind our respective section of the day's newspaper. Neither of us was a morning person and, needless to say, this wasn't the best time to communicate. Ergo, there was very little communication.

After the divorce, Ted got custody of the house and all it contained, plus the car, the neighbors, the community, the committees and the club. I was more than willing to leave the suburban palace he coveted, complete with court and attendants, and take a small but comfortable apartment near my office. By saving myself two hours of commuting a day I hoped to free some time and energy, finally, for myself.

So far, one year and six months later, there had been little productive use of that extra time. Most of the initial hurt had dissolved but there was still that twinge of pain whenever I thought about my years as Ted's doormat. Not that I resented Ted for the time he caused me to waste or for the tears I shed when he told me he was bored to death with me and wanted a divorce — even though he assured me that having all his bills finally paid had nothing to do with it.

Of course not.

In any event, I wasn't the type of woman who harbored resentments. Not me.

Besides, I'd break out in hives or suffer indigestion when, I mean if I did — so I overcame any possible thoughts of bitterness or revenge and set out to make my own life a better one.

Marsha's prattle on the open phone line brought me back to our conversation.

"Marsha, this is not crazy." I tried to defend my action. "A lot of women in my position are doing it."

"Trish — you see, I got it right — a lot of women in your position are crazy. Placing a classified ad for a man! What do you think you'll find?"

"Maybe something I lost, or maybe something I nevet had to begin with," I philosophically answered. "After all, this is just an extension of the old 'lost and found' columns. Besides, it's too late to argue the point. I've done it. I've placed a classified ad and it's scheduled to run in this afternoon's paper."

Marsha sighed, a sure sign she had all but given up hope. "What did your ad say?" she asked. "I've seen some very strange ads and can only hope you stayed within the bounds of good taste."

Not knowing whether to be amused or insulted, I decided amused would be the better tack. "Why, Marsha, I didn't know you read the classifieds." Score one for me, I thought, as my good friend hemmed and hawed her way through a few minutes explaining that she occasionally glanced at the section though never, of course, read — much less had any other interest — in the ads.

"I can assure you my ad was in the best of taste," I finally answered her original question after she wound down her encumbered explanations. "Here, I've a copy and I'll read it to you."

Sorting through the massive piles of paper on my desk I unerringly pulled just the right piece of paper from a stack of bills to be approved, inter-office memos, and tasks not yet even contemplated. My skill at desk-top filing was impeccable.

"Attractive and single female jazz dancer looking for male alto sax. Object, Jam sessions. Write Box 440 to set date for gig," I read my ad with renewed excitement. It was rather clever, I thought.

Stunned silence met the anticipated camaraderie. Finally, a weary voice said, "Patti, I mean Trish, you've lost it. That ad is absurd."

"I think it's great!"

"What does it mean?" Marsha, who always kept her closet hung in alphabetical order, asked.

"Well," I tried to explain. "What it means, or what I mean, is that I'm available and looking for a man to go out with. I love jazz and I thought I'd catch another jazz fan's eye."

"I'm afraid of what you might catch with that bait," Marsha dejectedly responded.

"In any event," I patiently continued, "the ad runs today and the answers go to a post office box. The newspaper will forward the answers in confidence, no one wil know my name and I get to pick the letters I want to answer. What could be safer?"

"I don't know," said Marsha, resigning herself to my fate. After a moment of thoughtfully and audibly chewing her celery stick, she added her finaì words on the subject. "Just be careful."

"I will," I promised.

The rest of the afternoon was spent moving papers from pile to pile, anticipating reading my ad, my very own ad, in the late afternoon paper.

It was routinely dropped off at my desk. I swiftly snatched up the daily edition with more enthusiasm than I'd shown over anything in the past year and a half. The mailroom clerk noticed my lunge but probably chalked it up to a sale at Clayton's Department Store — I hoped. As soon as the clerk was a discreet distance away I turned to the classified section.

There was my ad, third down in the second column. Good position, I thought. Not too pushy, like being first, yet not last and forlorn in the pack.

After carefully reading my ad for typos, not one thank goodness, I read the ads positioned before and after mine — as well as those adjacent in the columns on either side. Relief flooded through me when I realized mine was surrounded by mundane, mediocre and otherwise boring copy. I stood out like a jewel in the sun, a star in the crowd, a shining ray of hope amid the dullness surrounding me. I walked home on a cloud, felt light as a feather, whistled a happy tune and was otherwise feeling pretty jazzy.

A day or two and the world would be my oyster, they'd be lining up at my doorstep, I could take my pick of the city's most attractive and available bachelors. Ahh, to be beautiful, witty and desired!

"Who, me?" I said aloud as the fantasy burst (yes, like a bubble). Still giggling to myself over my flight into platitude lane I was, nonetheless, in a very good mood.

The next two days dragged on endlessly, and then came the weekend. My normally tedious routine of housework, shopping, exercise class and reading was all that was available to me to maintain any semblance of normalcy. A movie with Marsha might have helped pass the time but she was busy with a visiting aunt.

Monday dawned bright and cheerful, a sanguine smell to the early morning air. Today, I knew as soon as I opened my eyes, would be the day I would get the hundreds of letters responding to my clever ad. I'd answer only the best dozen or so, ignoring the ordinary and even slightly better than ordinary. My life would change when I got home that night.

The day went rather quickly. My office associates seemed to sense the excitement and offered me just enough of a challenge to let me handle my assignments with a flair. Almost too soon the day was over and I was home.

As I opened the downstairs door, the hall table for packages and magazines was in a direct line of sight. On the table lay three large envelopes. Rushing to reach the table, and catching my heel in the worn hall carpeting in the process, I quickly scooped all three packages up in my arms and headed for my own apartment door.

Fumbling with the key, I glanced at the corner of the first package, which was as far as I could see with my hands full. A return address in Kansas noticeably dampened my spirits. Walking back to the hall table, I replaced the top envelope. The second envelope, not that I looked, was for the young married couple in the upstairs east apartment and the third, and last, was for the retired gentleman in the apartment opposite me.

Dejected, nay — crushed I headed for my small mailbox. There was a slightly oversized envelope that I could see through the grid, and reaching in I saw it was not only for me but was from the newspaper.

Good things often come in small packages, I consoled myself, and, with my door key now ready, entered my apartment.

The small lamp I always kept lit to ward off any intruders glowed softly in the far corner of the combination living and dining room. After paying the lawyers for the divorce, which Ted had claimed was my financial responsibility — he would be forced to maintain the expensive house and property — my decorating budget had been severely limited. Eventually, when the three years loan was paid, I would replace the cinderblock-and-wood bookshelves and the Salvation Army couch. My dinette set had been our kitchen set, Ted's and mine, and he had let me have it.

Putting my coat and purse in the bedroom, which did contain a bed, I carried the envelope back to the dining table. Opening it, I coolly assured myself, would wait until after I started dinner. I did this with great alacrity — tearing open the frozen food package and skillfully popping it into the oven.

Pouring myself a light scotch and soda, I tuned the radio to my favorite classical music station, stretched out on the overstuffed, slightly lumpy sofa and opened the envelope.

Three letters, all addressed to the box number I used in my ad, fell into my lap.

The one on top looked good right away. Creamy-colored, heavy stationery, of obvious good quality, it immediately stood out. Putting the other two aside, I tore the heavy envelope open. A color-coordinated sheet of paper was neatly folded in thirds, not one careless crease which I found of great importance, and contained a symmetrically balanced and well penned letter.

What it said was also wonderful. Signed "Albert," it was addressed to "Dear Jazz Baby," and he had picked up exactly on the tone I was hoping my ad would convey. "The high notes that Miles Davis can reach are just the beginning of the heights I would take you to," the letter started. He talked about Paul Horn and Coltrane (both John and Alice) and how he would travel with me on their musical journeys. Mentioning an upcoming Keith Jarrett "gig date," he assured me that if I called him I would never have to sing the blues. It was a wonderful letter and, heartened, I resolved to call him at the number listed first thing in the morning. It was the first time I ever mildly resented not being able to afford a phone at home.

Both the other envelopes were similar — standard size, standard quality paper, typed and with no return address. Picking one at random, I slit it open.

The second letter was awful. Suffice it to say that I crumpled it into a ball and tossed it towards the kitchen trash can as quickly as I could. I missed and wondered how long it would be before it was safe to pick it up and put it in the trash. There are some very sick people in this world.

Carefully looking at the third envelope for any clue as to its contents, and finding none, I realized I would have to open the letter.

It wasn't bad. Actually, it was quite charming when read on its own, but I found myself comparing it to the first wonderful letter. The gentleman who wrote the, and I was sure he was a gentleman because he addressed me as "Dear Jazz Lady," signed himself Edward.

Edward told of his lonely life, evenings spent alone with his music — in which jazz played an important part, he wrote — and his books. I could almost smell his pipe tobacco as I read, knowing he wore tweed jackets with suede-patched elbows and sat in a worn red leather armchair. Edward asked that I not call, that he would prefer a return letter. That although he was home by the phone every night he would prefer learning about the inner me before hearing my voice. That way, he wrote, we would have something to talk about when we met.

Edward also asked that I write him care of a post office box until we got to know each other better. I was impressed with his prudence and resolved to secure a postal box for myself the very next day so that I could do likewise. A man who values his privacy now, I thought, would be all that much more worth the effort.

Perfect, I thought, whipping over to the shelf where my stationery rested. I get to talk to Albert tomorrow and write Edward at the same time. Wait until I tell Marsha. I might even treat at our weekly Friday lunch just to see the expression on her face.

Two days hence the salad bar was crowded but we found a small table in the back. Waiting to order our drinks before filling up at the salad bar, Marsha's curiosity won out over my reticence to open the subject and gloat.

"Well, Trish — I've finally got the hang of that," she cautiously opened the conversation, "have you been swamped with men from the ad?" I thought I caught a sarcastic tone in her voice but being the bearer of good news I could afford to be generous and ignore any dig.

"As a matter of fact, Marsha," I coolly replied, lighting a cigarette but screwing up the inhale, "I've a date tonight. His name is Albert and he sounds absolutely divine." I took another drag of the cigarette, getting it right this time, and practiced a sultry smile.

"Put that thing out," snapped my friend. "You've never smoked, you look foolish trying and I don't know what kind of expression of your face makes, you look like you have indigestion."

Realizing she was probably right, but could have phrased it better, I put out the cigarette and returned to my normal lopsided smile.

"He does sound interesting. His letter was fantastic," I gushed as I dug to retrieve it from my oversized purse. Handing it over, I could see she was impressed by the stationery. "I called him this morning and he suggested a drink after work."

"As long as it's a public bar with lots of people around I guess it will be okay," Marsha said as she scanned his letter. "Well, he doesn't sound like a nut case from this," she conceded as she returned the letter to me. "Was this the only response?"

"Heavens, no," I said with what I hoped was just the right degree of aloofness. "There were scads of letters. I haven't even opened all of them yet." I crossed my fingers under the table, hoping there was finally another envelope waiting for me so I wouldn't be a complete liar. After the three letters on Monday my mailbox had completely dried up — only bills and circulars from the laundromat found their way into its federally protected sanctuary.

Marsha studied me closely, her face a serene mask. "Were the other letters as interesting as this one?"

"There were other very interesting letters, but I liked this one the best. It struck just the right chord, if you know what I mean. He must be so responsive to pick up on the jazz theme the way he did and he's obviously trying to please me." This was also truth, I assured myself.

"Did you call any others?" Marsha asked, the barest flicker of interest showing in her eyes.

"Actually, I wrote one other. That should be enough for now. Next week I can contact more — that is, if one of these hasn't swept me off my feet."

"You wrote back? That means you gave him your address to write to." Alarm had crept into Marsha's voice. "You don't know if he's a homicidal maniac who'll come after you in the middle of the night."

"Not to worry, Marsha, you don't think I'd be that foolish? Of course I took out a postal box and I'm not even using my real last name," I answered but neglected to add that I wrote him at his postal box.

"That's quite clever of you," my friend acknowledged. "I don't think I'll worry half as much knowing that you're taking precautions and approaching this wisely. Actually," Marsha leaned forward and dropped her voice to a conspiratorial hush, "ever since you told me what you did, well, I've been thinking about it.

It's not such an awful idea. And you seem to be doing so well."

To my credit, I didn't laugh at her. Nor did I tell her that I'd actually met Albert last night, the same day I called him. He was free for the evening and after I met him I realized why. They say that for everyone there is someone else, somewhere. I'm sure that's so, even for Albert, but there wasn't a chance in the world that someone was me.

That's not terribly nice and maybe not fair of me but I was just so disappointed when this wisp of a man sat down next to me. His forehead was level with my breast bone and I must have out-weighed him by fifty pounds — and I'm barely a size eight. Hope springs eternal, I thought, and at least I know he has a great mind.

Albert finally admitted, after almost an hour of hemming and hawing his way through some semblance of conversation, that he'd never listened to any music, much less jazz, in his life — unless you count commercial jingles on television. His roommate had helped him with the letter. A surge of hope hit me when he said that and I asked him about his roommate. It turned out to be his 80 year old uncle. I kept looking for something charming about him to hang on to but his conversation centered on his pet turtles, sit-com reruns (I've heard sit-com chatter done well but this wasn't one of those times) and his uncle's diet.

Marsha's words kept pouring out and I realized I hadn't been paying attention. Catching a phrase about her seeking new ho-rizons I breathed easier, knowing I hadn't missed much. She was working herself up to placing a classified ad and I was her sounding board.

"Of course it's a good idea, you don't think I'd ever do anything foolish?" I asked, all wide-eyed and sincere. Our drinks long gone, I curtailed further conversation and headed up toward the salad bar to fill up on our weekly allotment of chick peas and bean sprouts. Our munching was interrupted only by the barest bits of gossip.

Exchanging dutiful pecks on the cheek, we were heading back to our respective cubicles to finish the week's work. "Don't forget to tel me how it works out with Albert," Marsha gushed, "and let me know what happens with Edward. It's really so exciting."

Promising her anything until I could get my story straight, I headed back to work and consoled myself with the thought that Edward might very well have answered my letter by now and maybe I would have something interesting to tell her. I had until Monday before I reported in to Marsha and that should be enough time to come up with at least one interesting tidbit.

Encouraged, I decided to stop at the post office before I returned to the office. It was there, waiting for me.

A plain white envelope, like before, but this time I could have sworn I recognized the typewriter's peculiarities. I asked myself if it was because I felt I was already getting to know this man, but I forced myself to logically dismiss the thought as a touch too romantic. I was right, though, and it was a letter from Edward. He was, after all, the only person who knew my postal box number.

The afternoon flew by. He wanted to meet me. He even named a time and a place — Saturday night at 8 in the Gotham Hotel's lounge. A little more than twenty-four hours from now, twenty-nine at this exact moment, and I would be sitting next to the man of — maybe — my dreams. He described himself and I knew I'd recognize him anywhere. About 6 feet, sandy-brown hair and, I knew it all along, smoking a pipe.

Fortunately I'd included a description of myself in my letter which would be enough for him to know that I was the right person when I approached him — that is, if I ran over to Clayton's Department Store first thing in the morning and had my hair rinsed red, a full make-up scheduled and bought the slim skirt with the slit up the side, I might just pull it off.

I did. Saturday night came quickly after the day's activities but I was ready. Entering the Gotham lobby I paused for effect and was pleased to see that I did — have one, I mean. Heads turned. The exercise classes, the blue slit-skirt, the matching soft clinging sweater, perfectly accented by my favorite silk scarf stick-pinned to drape gracefully at my throat, and my mane of glowing red hair all added up to the "very attractive, trim and dynamic red-head" just as I had described myself.

I knew who he was the minute I entered the lounge. Sitting at the bar with his back to the door, his wonderful broad shoulders perfectly filled the tweed jacket, the aromatic clouds of pipe smoke seemed to fill the room with a heady perfume all its own. Quickly crossing the room, I reached out and touched his arm. He turned to face me, a smile frozen on his face.

"Patti."

"Ted."

"What are you doing here?"

"I'm meeting someone," I barely said, searching the rest of the room for my Edward.

"So am I."

"I'm sure Edward will be here in a minute, so I'll just leave you to wait."

His eyes seemed to roll upward in his head, the whites

showing under his half closed lids.

"Oh, no! You're Trish."

We looked at each other. The silence that followed was deafening.

"Look," he graciously began, "we've obviously gotten ourselves into a stew here. Why not at least join me for a drink?"

Welcoming the drink, I slid into the seat next to Ted and ordered a double scotch and water and, in a moment of reprisal, named Chivas Regal. Let him pick up the check. The drink was most helpful and immediately warmed me to the almost humorous situation in which I now found myself. By the end of the third drink we both found ourselves laughing about our cleverly disguised correspondence, how we both had revised our names to reflect our new "selves" and, oddly enough, how we both were interested in meeting someone new.

Ted, or Edward I should say, told me he'd been lonely. My disbelief must have been apparent because he hastened to fill me in on his life for the last year and a half.

"Patti, I mean Trish — you really look terrific, I barely recognized you — it hasn't been easy," he confided. "A lot of our neighbors were breaking up and the old party circuit just seemed to fall apart. George Hathaway, you remember George, moved in with me after Helen threw him out and we've been two bachelors, eating bar food and staying home most of the time."

To say I found this hard to believe was an understatement but, after more than five years living with Ted, I knew Edward was telling me the truth.

"Wait until I get home and tell George what happened tonight," he laughed in an odd deprecating way. "I told him I had a hot date with this gal I met last week. I didn't have the nerve to tell him I answered an ad."

"You don't have to tell him," I said, trying to console. "Just tell him we had a terrific time."

A crooked smile played at Edward's terrific mouth. "Maybe I will. How about another drink?"

Feeling woozy, I glanced at my watch and seeing it was after ten o'clock, realized that, true to form, Ted wouldn't spring for dinner and I'd better get myself home while I was still able. I murmured excuses and started to pull my purse towards me.

"Wait, I'll drive you home," Edward offered.

It was, at the moment, a good offer and one which I accepted. Waiting for him to settle the bill, which he did very slowly — as if to give me a chance to pitch in, fat chance — I touched up my new Brilliant Red lipstick. My reflection in the compact mirror told me that full cosmetics and a henna rinse were things I should really do more often — enough of this mouse brown haired lady.

The cool night air was welcome and sobering. Looking around the small lot I couldn't find our, I mean Ted's, white sedan. Guessing what I was looking for, Edward steered me to a brand new low and sleek shiny green two-seated sports car. An expensive looking sports car.

"It's brand new," he said. "What do you think?"

Flustered, I had to admit it was gorgeous. "I guess you can afford a car like this now, not being married and with a paying roommate," I said.

"I traded in the sedan last year and only have three years to go on the payments," he boasted. "It was expensive, but what the hell, I'm worth it."

Ted, and it was Ted talking now, pushed me against his prize vehicle, bending me backwards over the low roof, with only a well placed knee saving me from being ground into the maxi-waxed hood.

"Listen, Trish, I was thinking," he slurred in my ear as I maneuvered out from under him. "You're looking real good now. Why don't you move back in with me? We don't even have to get married this time. We're both looking for someone, right, and we're used to each other. And there's the car payments . . ."

I saw red. Three more years of car payments. Another year and a half still owed on the lawyers' loan. Good old doormat Patti. I still don't remember pulling the pin from my scarf and sticking it deep into his inner ear. I do remember saying something appropriate at the moment, that is, about sticking it in his ear and I also remember Ted falling at my feet — but we'd had a lot to drink. Come to think of it, there was a small drop of blood clinging to my stick pin when I wiped it clean on his suit.

When the police came late Sunday afternoon I had already washed the red out of my hair. Once a femme fatal might just be one time too many. I was sitting around reading a rather thick book — on about page 50 — dressed in comfortable jeans and sweat-shirt; I had my own scrubbed clean face back on.

The police lieutenant was sympathetic, having to tell me my ex-husband had been killed in the Gotham parking lot. At first I caught a hard glint in his eye, especially when he asked me where, and how, I spent my Saturday night.

Gesturing to my book, I apologized for being home, alone, reading. The glint in his eye almost gave off a spark at the thought, my worst fear closing in on me like heavy fog.

About to stammer something like a confession, I quickly shut my open mouth when I saw the tall, dark and handsome policeman close his notebook. His sardonic smile melted my heart when he told me he could hardly believe an attractive woman like myself had spent Saturday night at home alone. But his notebook was closed, so I put on the sultry smile I'd practiced on Marsha and blushed.

The best part was that when he looked at me, that glint was now taking on a different context. He asked me if I had any idea who Ted (as I referred to him, of course) had been with. The bartender described a knock-out redhead and Ted's friend and roommate George gave her name as Trish. George said that Edward (as he referred to him, of course) had been dating her for a few weeks.

I was very sorry I couldn't help him. ✗

Jean Paiva (1944–1989) had many careers: corporate communications, cable TV marketer, trade journalist, cofounder and editor of Crawdaddy *magazine, and fantasy writer. NAL Onyx published two novels by Jean,* The Lilith Factor *and* The Last Gamble. *Only one short story was published during her tragically brief life, "Just Idle Chatter," in Kathryn Ptacek's* Women of Darkness II, *but she left nearly a dozen complete short stories behind, and this magazine is committed to printing them all. "Had she lived, she would have been one of the great dark fantasists," Tanith Lee writes.*

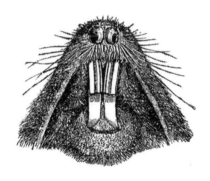

Sherlock Holmes Classic:
THE "GLORIA SCOTT"

by Arthur Conan Doyle

"**I** have some papers here," said my friend Sherlock Holmes as we sat one winter's night on either side of the fire, "which I really think, Watson, that it would be worth your while to glance over. These are the documents in the extraordinary case of the *Gloria Scott*, and this is the message which struck Justice of the Peace Trevor dead with horror when he read it."

He had picked from a drawer a little tarnished cylinder, and, undoing the tape, he handed me a short note scrawled upon a half-sheet of slate-grey paper.

> The supply of game for London is going steadily up [it ran]. Head-keeper Hudson, we believe, has been now told to receive all orders for fly-paper and for preservation of your hen-pheasant's life.

As I glanced up from reading this enigmatical message, I saw Holmes chuckling at the expression upon my face.

"You look a little bewildered," said he.

"I cannot see how such a message as this could inspire horror. It seems to me to be rather grotesque than otherwise."

"Very likely. Yet the fact remains that the reader, who was a fine, robust old man, was knocked clean down by it as if it had been the butt end of a pistol."

"You arouse my curiosity," said I. "But why did you say just now that there were very particular reasons why I should study this case?"

"Because it was the first in which I was ever engaged."

I had often endeavoured to elicit from my companion what had first turned his mind in the direction of criminal research, but had never caught him before in a communicative humour. Now he sat forward in his armchair and spread out the documents upon his knees. Then he lit his pipe and sat for some time smoking and turning them over.

"You never heard me talk of Victor Trevor?" he asked. "He was the only friend I made during the two years I was at college. I was never a very sociable fellow, Watson, always rather fond of moping in my rooms and working out my own little methods of thought, so that I never mixed much with the men of my year. Bar fencing and boxing I had few athletic tastes, and then my line of study was quite distinct from that of the other fellows, so that we had no points of contact at all. Trevor was the only man I knew, and that only through the accident of his bull terrier freezing on to my ankle one morning as I went down to chapel.

"It was a prosaic way of forming a friendship, but it was effective. I was laid by the heels for ten days, and Trevor used to come in to inquire after me. At first it was only a minute's chat but soon his visits lengthened, and before the end of the term we were close friends. He was a hearty, full-blooded fellow, full of spirits and energy, the very opposite to me in most respects, but we had some subjects in common, and it was a bond of union when I found that he was as friendless as I. Finally he invited me down to his father's place at Donnithorpe, in Norfolk, and I accepted his hospitality for a month of the long vacation.

"Old Trevor was evidently a man of some wealth and consideration, a J. P., and a landed proprietor. Donnithorpe is a little hamlet just to the north of Langmere, in the country of the Broads. The house was an old-fashioned, widespread, oak-beamed brick building, with a fine lime-lined avenue leading up to it. There was excellent wild-duck shooting in the fens, remarkably good fishing, a small but select library, taken over, as I understood, from a former occupant, and a tolerable cook, so that he would be a fastidious man who could not put in a pleasant month there.

"Trevor senior was a widower, and my friend his only son. There had been a daughter, I heard, but she had died of diphtheria while on a visit to Birmingham. The father interested me extremely. He was a man of little culture, but with a considerable amount of rude strength, both physically and mentally. He knew hardly any books, but he had travelled far, had seen much of the world, and had remembered all that he had learned. In person he was a thick-set, burly man with a shock of grizzled hair, a brown, weather-beaten face, and blue eyes which were keen to the verge of fierceness. Yet he had a reputation for kindness and charity on the countryside, and was noted for the leniency of his sentences from the bench.

"One evening, shortly after my arrival, we were sitting over a glass of port after dinner, when young Trevor began to talk about those habits of observation and inference which I had already formed into a system, although I had not yet appreciated the part which they were to play in my life. The old man evidently thought that his son was exaggerating in his description of one or two trivial feats which I had performed.

"'Come, now, Mr Holmes,' said he, laughing good-humouredly. 'I'm an excellent subject, if you can deduce anything from me.'

"'I fear there is not very much,' I answered. 'I might suggest that you have gone about in fear of some personal attack within the last twelvemonth.'

"The laugh faded from his lips, and he stared at me in great surprise.

"'Well, that's true enough,' said he. 'You know, Victor,' turning to his son, 'when we broke up that poaching gang they swore to knife us, and Sir Edward Holly has actually been attacked. I've always been on my guard since then, though I have no idea how you know it.'

"'You have a very handsome stick,' I answered. 'By the inscription I observed that you had not had it more than a year. But you have taken some pains to bore the head of it and pour melted lead into the hole so as to make it a formidable weapon. I argued that you would not take such precautions unless you had some danger to fear.'

"'Anything else?' he asked, smiling.

"'You have boxed a good deal in your youth.'

"'Right again. How did you know it? Is my nose knocked a little out of the straight?'

"'No,' said I. 'It is your ears. They have the peculiar flattening and thickening which marks the boxing man.'

"'Anything else?'

"'You have done a good deal of digging by your callosities.'

"'Made all my money at the gold fields.'

"'You have been in New Zealand.'

"'Right again.'

"'You have visited Japan.'

"'Quite true.'

"'And you have been most intimately associated with someone whose initials were J. A., and whom you afterwards were eager to entirely forget.'

"Mr. Trevor stood slowly up, fixed his large blue eyes upon me with a strange wild stare, and then pitched forward, with his face among the nutshells which strewed the cloth, in a dead faint.

"You can imagine, Watson, how shocked both his son and I were. His attack did not last long, however, for when we undid his collar and sprinkled the water from one of the finger-glasses over his face, he gave a gasp or two and sat up.

"'Ah, boys,' said he, forcing a smile, 'I hope I haven't frightened you. Strong as I look, there is a weak place in my heart, and it does not take much to knock me over. I don't know how you manage this, Mr Holmes, but it seems to me that all the detectives of fact and of fancy would be children in your hands. That's your line of life, sir, and you may take the word of a man who has seen something of the world.'

"And that recommendation, with the exaggerated estimate of my ability with which he prefaced it, was, if you will believe me, Watson, the very first thing which ever made me feel that a profession might be made out of what had up to that time been the merest hobby. At the moment, however, I was too much concerned at the sudden illness of my host to think of anything else.

"'I hope that I have said nothing to pain you?' said I.

"'Well, you certainly touched upon rather a tender point.

Might I ask how you know, and how much you know?' He spoke now in a half-jesting fashion, but a look of terror still lurked at the back of his eyes.

"'It is simplicity itself,' said I. 'When you bared your arm to draw that fish into the boat I saw that J. A. had been tattooed in the bend of the elbow. The letters were still legible, but it was perfectly clear from their blurred appearance, and from the staining of the skin round them, that efforts had been made to obliterate them. It was obvious, then, that those initials had once been very familiar to you, and that you had afterwards wished to forget them.'

"'What an eye you have!' he cried with a sigh of relief. 'It is just as you say. But we won't talk of it. Of all ghosts the ghosts of our old loves are the worst. Come into the billiard-room and have a quiet cigar.'

"From that day, amid all his cordiality, there was always a touch of suspicion in Mr Trevor's manner towards me. Even his son remarked it. 'You've given the governor such a turn,' said he, 'that he'll never be sure again of what you know and what you don't know.' He did not mean to show it, I am sure, but it was so strongly in his mind that it peeped out at every action. At last I became so convinced that I was causing him uneasiness that I drew my visit to a close. On the very day, however, before I left, an incident occurred which proved in the sequel to be of importance.

"We were sitting out upon the lawn on garden chairs, the three of us, basking in the sun and admiring the view across the Broads, when a maid came out to say that there was a man at the door who wanted to see Mr Trevor.

"'What is his name?' asked my host.

"'He would not give any.'

"'What does he want, then?'

"'He says that you know him, and that he only wants a moment's conversation.'

"'Show him round here.' An instant afterwards there appeared a little wizened fellow with a cringing manner and a shambling style of walking. He wore an open jacket, with a splotch of tar on the sleeve, a red-and-black check shirt, dungaree trousers, and heavy boots badly worn. His face was thin and brown and crafty, with a perpetual smile upon it, which showed an irregular line of yellow teeth, and his crinkled hands were half closed in a way that is distinctive of sailors. As he came slouching across the lawn I heard Mr. Trevor make a sort of hiccoughing noise in his throat, and, jumping out of his chair, he ran into the house. He was back in a moment, and I smelt a strong reek of brandy as he passed me.

"'Well, my man,' said he. 'What can I do for you?'

"The sailor stood looking at him with puckered eyes, and with the same loose-lipped smile upon his face.

'You don't know me?' he asked.

'Why, dear me, it is surely Hudson,' said Mr Trevor in a tone of surprise.

'Hudson it is, sir,' said the seaman. 'Why, it's thirty year and more since I saw you last. Here you are in your house, and me still picking my salt meat out of the harness cask.'

'Tut, you will find that I have not forgotten old times,' cried Mr Trevor, and, walking towards the sailor, he said something in a low voice. 'Go into the kitchen,' he continued out loud, 'and you will get food and drink. I have no doubt that I shall find you a situation.'

'Thank you, sir,' said the seaman, touching his forelock. 'I'm just off a two-yearer in an eight-knot tramp, short-handed at that, and I wants a rest. I thought I'd get it either with Mr Beddoes or with you.'

"'Ah!' cried Mr Trevor. 'You know where Mr Beddoes is?'

"'Bless you, sir, I know where all my old friends are,' said the fellow with a sinister smile, and he slouched off after the maid to the kitchen. Mr Trevor mumbled something to us about having been shipmate with the man when he was going back to the diggings, and then, leaving us on the lawn, he went indoors. An hour later, when we entered the house, we found him stretched dead drunk upon the dining-room sofa. The whole incident left a most ugly impression upon my mind, and I was not sorry next day to leave Donnithorpe behind me, for I felt that my presence must be a source of embarrassment to my friend.

"All this occurred during the first month of the long vacation. I went up to my London rooms, where I spent seven weeks working out a few experiments in organic chemistry. One day, however, when the autumn was far advanced and the vacation drawing to a close, I received a telegram from my friend imploring me to return to Donnithorpe, and saying that he was in great need of my advice and assistance. Of course I dropped everything and set out for the North once more.

"He met me with the dog-cart at the station, and I saw at a glance that the last two months had been very trying ones for him. He had grown thin and careworn, and had lost the loud, cheery manner for which he had been remarkable.

"'The governor is dying,' were the first words he said.

"'Impossible!' I cried. 'What is the matter?'

"'Apoplexy. Nervous shock. He's been on the verge all day. I doubt if we shall find him alive.'

"I was, as you may think, Watson, horrified at this unexpected news.

"'What has caused it?' I asked.

"'Ah, that is the point. Jump in and we can talk it over while we drive. You remember that fellow who came upon the evening before you left us?'

"'Perfectly.'

"'Do you know who it was that we let into the house that day?'

"'I have no idea.'

"'It was the devil, Holmes,' he cried.

"I stared at him in astonishment.

"'Yes, it was the devil himself. We have not had a peaceful hour since — not one. The governor has never held up his head from that evening, and now the life has been crushed out of him and his heart broken, all through this accursed Hudson.'

"'What power had he, then?'

"'Ah, that is what I would give so much to know. The kindly, charitable good old governor — how could he have fallen into the clutches of such a ruffian! But I am so glad that you have come, Holmes. I trust very much to your judgment and discretion, and I know that you will advise me for the best.'

"We were dashing along the smooth white country road, with the long stretch of the Broads in front of us glimmering in the red light of the setting sun. From a grove upon our left I could already see the high chimneys and the flagstaff which marked the squire's dwelling.

"'My father made the fellow gardener,' said my companion, 'and then, as that did not satisfy him, he was promoted to be butler. The house seemed to be at his mercy, and he wandered about and did what he chose in it. The maids complained of his drunken habits and his vile language. Then dad raised their wages all round to recompense them for the annoyance. The fellow would take the boat and my father's best gun and treat himself to little shooting trips. And all this with such a sneering, leering, insolent face that I would have knocked him down twenty times over if he had been a man of my own age. I tell you, Holmes, I have had to keep a tight hold upon myself all this time and now I am asking myself whether, if I had let myself go a little more, I might not have been a wiser man.

"'Well, matters went from bad to worse with us, and this animal Hudson became more and more intrusive, until at last, on his making some insolent reply to my father in my presence one day, I took him by the shoulders and turned him out of the room.

"He slunk away with a livid face and two venomous eyes which uttered more threats than his tongue could do. I don't know what passed between the poor dad and him after that, but the dad came to me next day and asked me whether I would mind apologizing to Hudson. I refused, as you can imagine, and asked my father how he could allow such a wretch to take such liberties with himself and his household.

"'Ah, my boy,' said he, 'it is all very well to talk, but you don't know how I am placed. But you shall know, Victor. I'll see that you shall know, come what may. You wouldn't believe harm of your poor old father, would you, lad?' He was very much moved and shut himself up in the study all day, where I could see through the window that he was writing busily.

"That evening there came what seemed to me to be a grand release, for Hudson told us that he was going to leave us. He walked into the dining-room as we sat after dinner and announced his intention in the thick voice of a half-drunken man.

"'I've had enough of Norfolk,' said he. 'I'll run down to Mr Beddoes in Hampshire. He'll be as glad to see me as you were, I daresay.'

"'You're not going away in an unkind spirit, Hudson, I hope,' said my father with a tameness which made my blood boil.

"'I've not had my 'pology,' said he sulkily, glancing in my direction.

"'Victor, you will acknowledge that you have used this worthy fellow rather roughly,' said the dad, turning to me.

"'On the contrary, I think that we have both shown extraordinary patience towards him,' I answered.

"'Oh, you do, do you?' he snarled. 'Very good, mate. We'll see about that!'

"He slouched out of the room and half an hour afterwards left the house, leaving my father in a state of pitiable nervousness. Night after night I heard him pacing his room, and it was just as he was recovering his confidence that the blow did at last fall."

"'And how?' I asked eagerly.

"'In a most extraordinary fashion. A letter arrived for my father yesterday evening, bearing the Fordingham postmark. My father read it, clapped both his hands to his head, and began running round the room in little circles like a man who has been driven out of his senses. When I at last drew him down on to the sofa, his mouth and eyelids were all puckered on one side, and I saw that he had a stroke. Dr Fordham came over at once. We put him to bed, but the paralysis has spread, he has shown no sign of returning consciousness, and I think that we shall hardly find him alive.'

"'You horrify me, Trevor!' I cried. 'What then could have been in this letter to cause so dreadful a result?'

"'Nothing. There lies the inexplicable part of it. The message was absurd and trivial. Ah, my God, it is as I feared!'

"As he spoke we came round the curve of the avenue and saw in the fading light that every blind in the house had been drawn down. As we dashed up to the door, my friend's face convulsed with grief, a gentleman in black emerged from it.

"'When did it happen, doctor?' asked Trevor.

"'Almost immediately after you left.'

"'Did he recover consciousness?'

"'For an instant before the end.'

"'Any message for me?'

"'Only that the papers were in the back drawer of the Japanese cabinet.'

"My friend ascended with the doctor to the chamber of death while I remained in the study, turning the whole matter over and over in my head, and feeling as sombre as ever I had done in my life. What was the past of this Trevor, pugilist, traveller, and gold-digger, and how had he placed himself in the power of this acid-faced seaman? Why, too, should he faint at an allusion to the half-effaced initials upon his arm and die of fright when he had a letter from Fordingham? Then I remembered that Fordingham was in Hampshire, and that this Mr Beddoes, whom the seaman had gone to visit and presumably to blackmail, had also been mentioned as living in Hampshire. The letter, then, might either come from Hudson, the seaman, saying that he had betrayed the guilty secret which appeared to exist, or it might come from Beddoes, warning an old confederate that such a betrayal was imminent. So far it seemed clear enough. But then how could this letter be trivial and grotesque, as described by the son? He must have misread it. If so, it must have been one of those ingenious secret codes which mean one thing while they seem to mean another. I must see this letter. If there was a hidden meaning in it, I was confident that I could pluck it forth. For an hour I sat pondering over it in the gloom, until at last a weeping maid brought in a lamp, and close at her heels came my friend Trevor, pale but composed, with these very papers which lie upon my knee held in his grasp. He sat down opposite to me, drew the lamp to the edge of the table, and handed me a short note scribbled, as you see, upon a single sheet of grey paper.

'The supply of game for London is going steadily up,' it ran. 'Head-keeper Hudson, we believe, has been now told to receive all orders for fly-paper and for preservation of your hen-pheasant's life.'

"I daresay my face looked as bewildered as yours did just now when first I read this message. Then I reread it very carefully. It was evidently as I had thought, and some secret meaning must lie buried in this strange combination of words. Or could it be that there was a prearranged significance to such phrases as 'fly-paper' and 'hen-pheasant'? Such a meaning would be arbitrary and could not be deduced in any way. And yet I was loath to believe that this was the case, and the presence of the word Hudson seemed to show that the subject of the message was as I had guessed, and that it was from Beddoes rather than the sailor. I tried it backward, but the combination 'life pheasant's hen' was not encouraging. Then I tried alternate words, but neither 'the of for' nor 'supply game London' promised to throw any light upon it.

"And then in an instant the key of the riddle was in my hands, and I saw that every third word, beginning with the first, would give a message which might well drive old Trevor to despair.

"It was short and terse, the warning, as I now read it to my companion:

"'The game is up. Hudson has told all. Fly for your life.'

"Victor Trevor sank his face into his shaking hands. 'It must be that, I suppose,' said he. 'This is worse than death, for it means disgrace as well. But what is the meaning of these "headkeepers" and "hen-pheasants"?'

"'It means nothing to the message, but it might mean a good deal to us if we had no other means of discovering the sender. You see that he has begun by writing "The . . . game . . . is," and so on. Afterwards he had, to fulfil the prearranged cipher, to fill in any two words in each space. He would naturally use the first words which came to his mind, and if there were so many which referred to sport among them, you may be tolerably sure that he is either an ardent shot or interested in breeding. Do you know anything of this Beddoes?'

"'Why, now that you mention it,' said he, 'I remember that my poor father used to have an invitation from him to shoot over his preserves every autumn.'

"'Then it is undoubtedly from him that the note comes,' said I.

'It only remains for us to find out what this secret was which the sailor Hudson seems to have held over the heads of these two wealthy and respected men.'

"'Alas, Holmes, I fear that it is one of sin and shame!' cried my friend. 'But from you I shall have no secrets. Here is the statement which was drawn up by my father when he knew that the danger from Hudson had become imminent. I found it in the Japanese cabinet, as he told the doctor. Take it and read it to me, for I have neither the strength nor the courage to do it myself.'

"These are the very papers, Watson, which he handed to me, and I will read them to you, as I read them in the old study that night to him. They are endorsed outside, as you see, 'Some particulars of the voyage of the bark *Gloria Scott*, from her leaving Falmouth on the 8th October, 1855, to her destruction in N. Lat. 15 degrees 20'. W. Long. 25 degrees 14', on Nov. 6th.' It is in the form of a letter, and runs in this way.

"'My dear, dear son, now that approaching disgrace begins to darken the closing years of my life, I can write with all truth and honesty that it is not the terror of the law, it is not the loss of my position in the county, nor is it my fall in the eyes of all who have known me, which cuts me to the heart; but it is the thought that you should come to blush for me — you who love me and who have seldom, I hope, had reason to do other than respect me. But if the blow falls which is forever hanging over me, then I should wish you to read this, that you may know straight from me how far I have been to blame. On the other hand, if all should go well (which may kind God Almighty grant!), then, if by any chance this paper should be still undestroyed and should fall into your hands, I conjure you, by all you hold sacred, by the memory of your dear mother, and by the love which has been between us, to hurl it into the fire and to never give one thought to it again.

"'If then your eye goes on to read this line, I know that I shall already have been exposed and dragged from my home, or, as is more likely, for you know that my heart is weak, be lying with my tongue sealed forever in death. In either case the time for suppression is past, and every word which I tell you is the naked truth, and this I swear as I hope for mercy.

"'My name, dear lad, is not Trevor. I was James Armitage in my younger days, and you can understand now the shock that it was to me a few weeks ago when your college friend addressed me in words which seemed to imply that he had surprised my secret. As Armitage it was that I entered a London banking-house, and as Armitage I was convicted of breaking my country's laws, and was sentenced to transportation. Do not think very harshly of me, laddie. It was a debt of honour, so called, which I had to pay, and I used money which was not my own to do it, in the certainty that I could replace it before there could be any possibility of its being missed. But the most dreadful ill-luck pursued me. The money which I had reckoned upon never came to hand, and a premature examination of accounts exposed my deficit. The case might have been dealt leniently with, but the laws were more harshly administered thirty years ago than now, and on my twenty-third birthday I found myself chained as a felon with thirty-seven other convicts in the 'tween-decks of the bark Gloria Scott, bound for Australia.

"'It was the year '55, when the Crimean War was at its height, and the old convict ships had been largely used as transports in the Black Sea. The government was compelled, therefore, to use smaller and less suitable vessels for sending out their prisoners. The *Gloria Scott* had been in the Chinese tea-trade, but she was an old-fashioned, heavy-bowed, broad-beamed craft, and the new clippers had cut her out. She was a five-hundred-ton boat; and besides her thirty-eight jail-birds, she carried twenty-six of a crew, eighteen soldiers, a captain, three mates, a doctor, a chaplain, and four warders. Nearly a hundred souls were in her, all told, when we set sail from Falmouth.

"'The partitions between the cells of the convicts instead of being of thick oak, as is usual in convict-ships, were quite thin and frail. The man next to me, upon the aft side, was one whom I had particularly noticed when we were led down the quay. He was a young man with a clear, hairless face, a long, thin nose, and rather nut-cracker jaws. He carried his head very jauntily in the air, had a swaggering style of walking, and was above all else, remarkable for his extraordinary height. I don't think any of our heads would have come up to his shoulder, and I am sure that he could not have measured less than six and a half feet. It was strange among so many sad and weary faces to see one which was full of energy and resolution. The sight of it was to me like a fire in a snowstorm. I was glad, then, to find that he was my neighbour, and gladder still when, in the dead of the night, I heard a whisper close to my ear and found that he had managed to cut an opening in the board which separated us.

"'"Hullo, chummy!" said he, "what's your name, and what are you here for?"

"'I answered him, and asked in turn who I was talking with.

"'"I'm Jack Prendergast," said he, "and by God! you'll learn to bless my name before you've done with me."

"'I remembered hearing of his case, for it was one which had made an immense sensation throughout the country some time before my own arrest. He was a man of good family and of great ability, but of incurably vicious habits, who had by an ingenious system of fraud obtained huge sums of money from the leading London merchants.

""""Ha, ha! You remember my case!" said he proudly.

""""Very well', indeed."

""""Then maybe you remember something queer about it?"

""""What was that, then?"

""""I'd had nearly a quarter of a million, hadn't I?"

""""So it was said."

""""But none was recovered, eh?"

""""No."

""""Well, where d'ye suppose the balance is?" he asked.

""""I have no idea," said I.

""""Right between my finger and thumb," he cried. "By God! I've got more pounds to my name than you've hairs on your head. And if you've money, my son, and know how to handle it and spread it, you can do anything. Now, you don't think it likely that a man who could do anything is going to wear his breeches out sitting in the stinking hold of a rat-gutted beetle-ridden, mouldy old coffin of a China coaster. No, sir, such a man will look after himself and will look after his chums. You may lay to that! You hold on to him, and you may kiss the Book that he'll haul you through."

"'That was his style of talk, and at first I thought it meant nothing; but after a while, when he had tested me and sworn me in with all possible solemnity, he let me understand that there really was a plot to gain command of the vessel. A dozen of the prisoners had hatched it before they came aboard, Prendergast was the leader, and his money was the motive power.

""""I'd a partner," said he, "a rare good man, as true as a stock to a barrel. He's got the dibbs, he has, and where do you think he is at this moment? Why, he's the chaplain of this ship — the chaplain, no less! He came aboard with a black coat, and his papers right, and money enough in his box to buy the thing right up from keel to main-truck. The crew are his, body and soul. He could buy 'em at so much a gross with a cash discount, and he did it before ever they signed on. He's got two of the warders and Mereer, the second mate, and he'd get the captain himself, if he thought him worth it."

""""What are we to do, then?" I asked.

""""What do you think?" said he. "We'll make the coats of some of these soldiers redder than ever the tailor did."

""""But they are armed," said I.

""""And so shall we be, my boy. There's a brace of pistols for every mother's son of us; and if we can't carry this ship, with the crew at our back, it's time we were all sent to a young misses' boarding-school. You speak to your mate upon the left tonight, and see if he is to be trusted."

"'I did so and found my other neighbour to be a young fellow in much the same position as myself, whose crime had been forgery. His name was Evans, but he afterwards changed it, like myself, and he is now a rich and prosperous man in the south of England. He was ready enough to join the conspiracy, as the only means of saving ourselves, and before we had crossed the bay there were only two of the prisoners who were not in the secret. One of these was of weak mind, and we did not dare to trust him, and the other was suffering from jaundice and could not be of any use to us.

"'From the beginning there was really nothing to prevent us from taking possession of the ship. The crew were a set of ruffians, specially picked for the job. The sham chaplain came into our cells to exhort us, carrying a black bag, supposed to be full of tracts, and so often did he come that by the third day we had each stowed away at the foot of our beds a file, a brace of pistols, a pound of powder, and twenty slugs. Two of the warders were agents of Prendergast, and the second mate was his right-hand man. The captain, the two mates, two warders, Lieutenant Martin, his eighteen soldiers, and the doctor were all that we had against us. Yet, safe as it was, we determihed to neglect no precaution, and to make our attack suddenly by night. It came, however, more quickly than we expected, and in this way.

"'One evening, about the third week after our start, the doctor had come down to see one of the prisoners who was ill, and putting his hand down on the bottom of his bunk, he felt the outline of the pistols. If he had been silent he might have blown the whole thing, but he was a nervous little chap, so he gave a cry of surprise and turned so pale that the man knew what was up in an instant and seized him. He was gagged before he could give the alarm and tied down upon the bed. He had unlocked the door that led to the deck, and we were through it in a rush. The two sentries were shot down, and so was a corporal who came running to see what was the matter. There were two more soldiers at the door of the stateroom, and their muskets seemed not to be loaded, for they never fired upon us, and they were shot whi!e trying to fix their bayonets. Then we rushed on into the captain's cabin, but as we pushed open the door there was an explosion from within, and there he lay with his brains smeared over the chart of the Atlantic which was pinned upon the table, while the chaplain stood with a smoking pistol in his hand at his elbow. The two mates had both been seized by the crew, and the whole business seemed to be settled.

"'The stateroom was next the cabin, and we flocked in there and flopped down on the settees, all speaking together, for we were just mad with the feeling that we were free once more. There were lockers all round, and Wilson, the sham chaplain, knocked one of them in, and pulled out a dozen of brown sherry. We cracked off the necks of the bottles, poured the stuff out into tumblers, and were just tossing them off when in an instant without warning there came the roar of muskets in our ears, and the saloon was so full of smoke that we could not see across the table. When it cleared again the place was a shambles. Wilson and eight others were wriggling on the top of each other on the floor, and the blood and the brown sherry on that table turn me sick now when I think of it. We were so cowed by the sight that I think we should have given the job up if it had not been for Prendergast. He bellowed like a bull and rushed for the door with all that were left alive at his heels. Out we ran, and there on the poop were the lieutenant and ten of his men. The swing skylights above the saloon table had been a bit open, and they had fired on us through the slit. We got on them before they could load, and they stood to it like men; but we had the upper hand of them, and in five minutes it was all over. My God! was there ever a slaughter-house like that ship! Prendergast was like a raging devil, and he picked the soldiers up as if they had been children and threw them overboard alive or dead. There was one sergeant that was horribly wounded and yet kept on swimming for a surprising time until someone in mercy blew out his brains.

When the fighting was over there was no one left of our enemies except just the warders, the mates, and the doctor.

"'It was over them that the great quarrel arose. There were many of us who were glad enough to win back our freedom, and yet who had no wish to have murder on our souls. It was one thing to knock the soldiers over with their muskets in their hands, and it was another to stand by while men were being killed in cold blood. Eight of us, five convicts and three sailors, said that we would not see it done. But there was no moving Prendergast and those who were with him. Our only chance of safety lay in making a clean job of it, said he, and he would not leave a tongue with power to wag in a witness-box. It nearly came to our sharing the fate of the prisoners, but at last he said that if we wished we might take a boat and go. We jumped at the offer, for we were already sick of these blood-thirsty doings, and we saw that there would be worse before it was done. We were given a suit of sailor togs each, a barrel of water, two casks, one of junk and one of biscuits, and a compass. Prendergast threw us over a chart, told us that we were shiprecked mariners whose ship had foundered in

Lat. 15 degrees and Long. 25 degrees west, and then cut the painter and let us go.

"'And now I come to the most surprising part of my story, my dear son. The seamen had hauled the fore-yard aback during the rising, but now as we left them they brought it square again, and as there was a light wind from the north and east the bark began to draw slowly away from us. Our boat lay, rising and falling, upon the long, smooth rollers, and Evans and I, who were the most educated of the party, were sitting in the sheets working out our position and planning what coast we should make for. It was a nice question, for the Cape Verdes were about five hundred miles to the north of us, and the African coast about seven hundred to the east. On the whole, as the wind was coming round to the north, we thought that Sierra Leone might be best and turned our head in that direction, the bark being at that time nearly hull down on our starboard quarter. Suddenly as we looked at her we saw a dense black cloud of smoke shoot up from her, which hung like a monstrous tree upon the sky-line. A few seconds later a roar like thunder burst upon our ears, and as the smoke thinned away there was no sign left of the *Gloria Scott*. In an instant we swept the boat's head round again and pulled with all our strength for the place where the haze still trailing over the water marked the scene of this catastrophe.

"'It was a long hour before we reached it, and at first we feared that we had come too late to save anyone. A splintered boat and a number of crates and fragments of spars rising and falling on the waves showed us where the vessel had foundered; but there was no sign of life, and we had turned away in despair, when we heard a cry for help and saw at some distance a piece of wreckage with a man lying stretched across it. When we pulled him aboard the boat he proved to be a young seaman of the name of Hudson, who was so burned and exhausted that he could give us no account of what had happened until the following morning.

"'It seemed that after we had left, Prendergast and his gang had proceeded to put to death the five remaining prisoners. The two warders had been shot and thrown overboard, and so also had the third mate. Prendergast then descended into the 'tween-decks and with his own hands cut the throat of the unfortunate surgeon. There only remained the first mate, who was a bold and active man. When he saw the convict approaching him with the bloody knife in his hand he kicked off his bonds, which he had somehow contrived to loosen, and rushing down the deck he plunged into the after-hold. A dozen convicts, who descended with their pistols in search of him, found him with a match-box in his hand seated beside an open powder-barrel, which was one of the hundred carried on board, and swearing that he would blow all hands up if he were in any way molested. An instant later the explosion occurred, though Hudson thought it was caused by the misdirected bullet of one of the convicts rather than the mate's match. Be the cause what it may, it was the end of the *Gloria Scott* and of the rabble who held command of her.

'Such, in a few words, my dear boy, is the history of this terrible business in which I was involved. Next day we were picked up by the brig Hotspur, bound for Australia, whose captain found no difficulty in believing that we were the survivors of a passenger ship which had foundered. The transport ship *Gloria Scott* was set down by the Admiralty as being lost at sea, and no word has ever leaked out as to her true fate. After an excellent voyage the Hotspur landed us at Sydney, where Evans and I changed our names and made our way to the diggings, where, among the crowds who were gathered from all nations, we had no difficulty in losing our former identities. The rest I need not relate. We prospered, we travelled, we came back as rich colonials to England, and we bought country estates. For more than twenty years we have led peaceful and useful lives, and we hoped that our past was forever buried. Imagine, then, my feelings when in the seaman who came to us I recognized instantly the man who had been picked off the wreck. He had tracked us down somehow and had set himself to live upon our fears. You will understand now how it was that I strove to keep the peace with him, and you will in some measure sympathize with me in the fears which fill me, now that he has gone from me to his other victim with threats upon his tongue.'

66**U**nderneath is written in a hand so shaky as to be hardly legible, 'Beddoes writes in cipher to say H. has told all. Sweet Lord, have mercy on our souls!'

"That was the narrative which I read that night to young Trevor, and I think, Watson, that under the circumstances it was a dramatic one. The good fellow was heart-broken at it, and went out to the Terai tea planting, where I hear that he is doing well. As to the sailor and Beddoes, neither of them was ever heard of again after that day on which the letter of warning was written. They both disappeared utterly and completely. No complaint had been lodged with the police, so that Beddoes had mistaken a threat for a deed. Hudson had been seen lurking about, and it was believed by the police that he had done away with Beddoes and had fled. For myself I believe that the truth was exactly the opposite. I think that it is most probable that Beddoes, pushed to desperation and believing himself to have been already betrayed, had revenged himself upon Hudson, and had fled from the country with as much money as he could lay his hands on. Those are the facts of the case, Doctor, and if they are of any use to your collection, I am sure that they are very heartily at your service." ✗

IN THE NEXT ISSUE . . .

Coming in the second issue of
Sherlock Holmes Mystery Magazine!

FICTION BY

KIM NEWMAN

RON GOULART

PAULA VOLSKY

FEATURES BY

ARTHUR CONAN DOYLE

CRAIG SHAW GARDNER

LENNY PICKER

& many more!